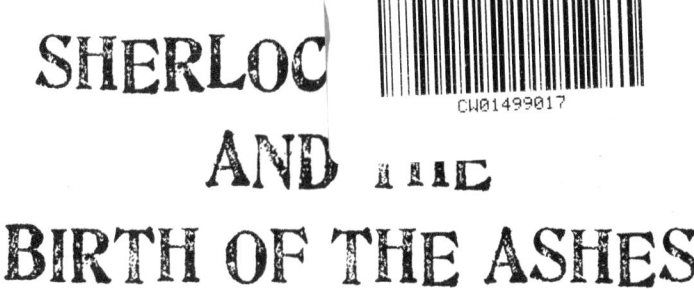

SHERLOCK
AND THE
BIRTH OF THE ASHES

The Cricket Mysteries of Sherlock Holmes Series – No 1.

Arunabha Sengupta

Max Books

First published in the UK in 2016 by Max Books

The right of Arunabha Sengupta to be identified as the Author of this work has been asserted by them in accordance with the Copyright, Designs and Patents Act 1988

A CIP catalogue record for this title is available from the British Library

ISBN: 978-0-9934872-0-0

Typeset and Design by Andrew Searle
Cover art by Austin Coutinho
Printed and bound by CPI Ltd

MAX BOOKS
Epworth House
34 Wellington Road
Nantwich Cheshire CW5 7BX
Tel: 01270 625278
Email: maxcricket@btinternet.com
www.max-books.co.uk

To Young Stamford

TESTIMONIALS

Stephen Chalke: "The whole idea of the book is a delight, and Sengupta has gone about the writing of it with great playfulness, which appealed to me very much. He has also mastered the language of a Holmes story and the period detail, not to mention all the cricketing history. I am most impressed."

David Frith: "I found it richly entertaining. I was on full alert throughout for historical inaccuracies - not necessarily expecting them, though the author's undertaking was fraught with risk. It rang true throughout. The fidelity to personality (such as we know it) was so pleasing. He knows his stuff."

ACKNOWLEDGEMENTS

I AM truly indebted to Tony Ring, one of the greatest PG Wodehouse scholars of the world. He demonstrated so wonderfully the degrees to which book collectors and connoisseurs can be steeped in their area of interest and live both fruitfully and blissfully, enjoying the great works of fiction while at the same time touching the lives of others. Although this book is not a Wodehousean pastiche, there were lots and lots of tips, details and pointers that I picked up from him.

Heartfelt gratitude to Stephen Chalke for providing his invaluable suggestions, critical comments as well as endless encouragement. It was indeed an honour to be guided by a cricket historian and writer of his stature.

Many many thanks to Susanna Kendall for her meticulous and thoroughly detailed editing and her scrupulous investigation into every minute fact documented in the novel to ensure factual and historical accuracy.

My sincere thanks to Bill Gordon, the librarian and the curator of the museum at The Oval cricket ground, for his help in identifying the books outlining the history and also the contemporary geography of this splendid sporting venue.

Neil Robinson, the library and research manager of MCC, also helped in the development for the book, with his patient assistance, especially by providing access to the collection of *Cricket – Weekly Record of the Game* dating back to 1882.

Special thanks to John McKenzie, to his excellent shop I have made many a happy visit, and the numerous times he helpfully pointed out books and authors that have been of immense assistance to the storyline. It was during one of the many lunches that we have had in the Italian restaurant near the shop that I mentioned to John that such a story could be written.

Plenty of help was extended along similar lines by Magnus Bowles of *Sportspages*.

A word of thanks as well for Caroline Warhurst, the Library and Information Services Manager of the London Transport Museum, for helping me find the details of transport and communication facilities in the great city towards the last part of the 19th century. Her diligent endeavours in compiling the mentions of cricket in the various transport publications of that period helped a lot in this volume and will be of invaluable assistance in the sequels as well.

Abhishek Mukherjee, my editor at Cricketcountry.com, was professionally thorough and quick in his review, and characteristically singular in his feedback. When, at one place, I missed the 'b' in Hornby— completely by accident, I assure you — his review comment was simply 'Aha!'.

Austin Coutinho has done a job with the cover illustration of the book as only an artist with his talent and cricketing background can.

And finally, Rumela, my wife, as usual went through the manuscript after the official edits to find if any error had slipped through.

CHAPTER I

THE GAME'S AFOOT

TO SHERLOCK Holmes, it was always *the* match.

I have seldom heard him mention it under any other name. In his eyes, *the* match eclipses and predominates the whole world of sports and games.

It was not that he felt any emotion akin to sporting excitement in relation to the Oval match. All emotions, including that particularly base one of frenzied sports enthusiasm, were abhorrent in his cold, precise but admirably balanced mind. He was, I have said it in other places, the most perfect reasoning and observing machine that the world has seen; but as a sports fan, he would have placed himself in a false position. He never spoke of the results of rugby or cricket, or even of fencing and boxing for which he possessed distinct talent, save with a gibe and a sneer. They were admirable entertainment for the observer — excellent for drawing the veil from men's motives and actions, most particularly the bookmakers and those men who staked for high sums. But for the trained reasoner to admit such intrusions into his own delicate and finely adjusted temperament was to introduce a distracting factor which might throw a doubt upon all his mental results.

And yet, there was but this one match for him, and that was the famous one that took place at the Kennington Oval in 1882.

Later, as representative matches became known as test matches, and then the 't' was capitalised to coin the term 'Test', he never used the word to describe the Oval match. And for ever after it was the only match that ever existed for him.

The match in question has remained a subject of curious interest, even beyond the exalted circles in which the noble game is discussed. There have been fresh developments, feats and scandals, but none have been able to eclipse the piquant details of the drama of that August afternoon. But, I have reasons to believe that the full facts have never been revealed to the general public, including the archivists and historians of the great game. As my friend Sherlock Holmes had a considerable share in clearing the matter up, I feel that no memoir of him would be complete without some little sketch of this remarkable episode.

The scandal surrounding the singular sequence of events had the potential to bring a great game, the game that has spread through our Empire, into disrepute. It was with these considerations in mind that in the years that followed, two noblemen who, for all intents and purposes, governed the game in the land, had my account of the events concealed. I was sworn to secrecy. Ultimately the tale was placed under the official seal for a century and a third thereof. It is with awe that I realise that these sinister events will come to light only in the fifteenth year of the new millennium, when, by all the laws of nature, neither my friend, nor I, nor any of those involved will be walking the earth to be affected or offended by the disclosures, being long entrenched, all of them, in the dark valley in which all paths meet.

The tale starts late on the Monday, 28th August, a damp dark evening with ominous clouds, when I alighted from the hansom cab, looked with some misgiving at the inky sky and made my way up the stairs of our common lodging in Baker Street. I found my friend seated in an armchair, his feet on another, flanks adorned by cushions and pillows from the various sofas and armchairs, smoking his pipe, the Persian slipper in which he kept his tobacco within arm's reach. Yet, in spite of his deportment, that of an emir settled on his eastern divan, he was dressed in his suit and waistcoat. Following the methods of deduction that I have always found so fascinating in my companion, I concluded that either he was expecting visitors or some had just left.

"Ah, Watson," said Holmes agreeably on seeing me, "Just the man I wanted to see. I suppose you can lay before me everything that happened at the cricket today that may be of interest."

The exciting events in the field had played on my mind throughout the return journey, especially in the way the Colonials, dismissed for a low score on a bumpy wicket on this murky day, had come back to nearly neutralise whatever advantage the great England cricketers had gained during the early afternoon. This they had achieved in spite of being without Joey Palmer, one of their main bowlers. Especially memorable was the menace of Spofforth, the way this bowler of demonic aspect had first laid low the wicket of our good Doctor and had then torn through the innings to reduce our advantage to a modest 38 runs. The weather had all the portents of remaining fickle and the devilry he could get up to with the ball on the morrow was a perplexing thought. I was about to launch into a detailed description of the day when I stopped.

"But Holmes, I never did tell you that I was going to the cricket!" I exclaimed.

Sherlock Holmes shook his head with a smile as he noticed my questioning glance. "Come now Watson, a public school athlete like you, one can be certain that Rugby Union for Blackheath is not the extent of your interest in sports. I have noticed you testing the recovery of your shoulder from the nasty effects of the Jezail bullet often enough by holding your walking stick and manoeuvring it in the way one might wield a cricket bat. Besides, for the past two days you have been overly anxious about the incessant rain, peering at the sky in the hope of sighting a patch of blue, even going to the extent of ignoring the old London adage 'rain before seven, gone by eleven' as you sat with a pensive expression at the breakfast table. Given the amount of attention the Australian cricketers have received in the newspapers recently, it was but the most basic conclusion that you were keen on the game not being washed out."

As I marvelled at his exceptional facility in deduction, Holmes continued, "Besides, you left home at a quarter to eleven, budgeting enough time to get to the Kennington Oval through the congested streets before the scheduled start — a clever ploy since even the extension of the underground has not quite made the roads easily navigable. In spite of the rain and resulting muddy streets, you have come back from your venture showing little residue of clay, silt or slush on your shoes. This confirms my assumption that you made your way to a sheltered place, stayed there for the duration of the day and made your way back. And you make your appearance as just enough time has elapsed after six o'clock to get you from the ground to Baker Street in the midst of the rushing omnibuses and cabs. I am sure, Watson, having missed the great match of 1880 by being away at the Afghan War, you could hardly bear to miss the excitement this time."

I had to admit that he was correct on all counts. "Really, Holmes, you continue to amaze me. Yet, since you ask, it was a most singular day's play. The Colonials, bowled out for 63 on a difficult, dicey wicket, struck back continuously till England lost all their men by the end of the day's play. We lead by 38, but with the weather likely to break at any moment who knows what is in store? Fred Spofforth, that demonic bowler, was virtually unplayable all through. But, Holmes, I've never known you to be keen on cricket, or any sport for that matter."

Holmes put his long fingers together and smiled. "Indeed I am not keen on sport, Watson, and the details of the match hold but scant interest for me. The behaviour of the crowd as they watch the game tells me a lot more of what I want to know. As I spent many of my formative years on the continent, I have had little introduction to the manly pursuits of the Englishman. To me a sport must carry with it the practical benefits which can stand a man in good stead in real life. Hence my preference for the art and science of pugilism and swordsmanship, and the ancient art of single stick if you categorise that martial form as sport. I also find so much armed conflict around the world that simulating a similar environment on the village green in the guise of a game seems redundant. Aside from that, I have often mentioned to you that facts are like furniture in our brains and inserting new necessitates hauling some of it to the lumber room to make the requisite space. Cricket, of all sports, is so designed as to clutter our heads with useless facts, with its many, many records and statistics; I prefer not to profess any interest for it."

It did seem strange to hear the most noble of sports referred to as a collection of useless facts. But I was used to the peculiarities of my friend in such regard. I have often listed his sphere of interests, and the areas of complete lack of interest in detail; such a mind cannot be traversed using the standard routes known to the common man.

He continued, "Yet, Watson, sports in general and specifically cricket hold singular interest for me. There is a murky strand of double dealing and vicious interests running through the pristine green fields of Victorian England. It is our duty to unravel it, and isolate, and expose every inch of it."

"Holmes," I exclaimed. "Without doubt you refer to the heinous activities of wagering and betting that used to go on in the old days of cricket. Wagering for high stakes is common today as well, but can it indeed be as sinister as you make it out to be?"

"Ah," said he. "*Omnibus locis fit caedes* and the same holds true for *alea*. However, we should be wiser by tomorrow. And here, I believe, is the man who will shed more light on the question. Stay here, Watson, for your somewhat plebeian interest in cricket can be of immense value to me."

There was the sound of hooves and wheels, and soon the boy in buttons came up to announce, to my great surprise, "Mr Charles Alcock."

CHAPTER 2

THE MAN OF SPORTS

THE MAN who walked in was impeccably dressed and of features so precisely familiar to me that I had to look twice to take in the presence of him in the flesh. Tall and broad-shouldered, he seemed larger and more imposing in real life than the pictures and distant sightings in the field had given me to assume, as is often the case with well-known men whose sketches and the occasional photographic prints were to be found everywhere.

"Why, it's Mr Alcock," I exclaimed, without restraint. I was in awe of the man, the force behind both football and cricket becoming international sports. He had been the secretary of the Football Association for as long as I could remember. Seven years ago, I had seen him captain England against Scotland at The Oval and score a goal in the 2-2 draw. He was also the Secretary of the Surrey County Club, for close to a decade, the most important man behind the great match between England and the

Colonials the first day of which I had just witnessed. Yet for all his accomplishments and the many offices that he held, and the iron-grey hair notwithstanding, he looked refreshingly youthful. Even the thick, greying moustache and his commanding air did not give the impression that he was more than in his late thirties.

"Indeed I am," he bowed gracefully.

"Good evening, Mr Charles Alcock," said Holmes. "I am Sherlock Holmes and this is my trusted friend Dr Watson. As you can make out from his exclamation, he has considerable knowledge of your accomplishments. He is occasionally good enough to help me with my cases and it will be most helpful to have him with us to discuss the matter at hand."

"I have been a great admirer ever since I saw you score that goal against Scotland on a slippery Oval in '75," I said.

Alcock waved his hand in the manner of the most modest of men. "I attribute it to the excellent corner kick and the skilful pass of Von Droop. From there it was just a few yards to the posts. The reason I am here today, though, has nothing to do with football and everything to do with cricket. That is the sport that is perhaps closer to my heart, even though my personal achievement in it has been far less than on the football field."

"But you did captain Middlesex," I protested.

"In precisely one match, my good sir, and I did not manage to get into the scorebook in that game. The moderate amount of success that I have indeed achieved as a cricketer has been curiously in foreign lands, in my younger, carefree days, representing France under an alias."

"Was it in Hamburg?" asked Sherlock Holmes.

Mr Charles Alcock went through the same reaction that I have seen in countless individuals who came across the powers of deduction of my companion. "How in the name of good fortune do you know that, Mr Holmes?"

"Your cuffs, my dear sir, or rather the cuff links that you wear. Today, of all days, is a great cricketing occasion with the Australians playing at The Oval. Given that you rushed here immediately after the day's play, hurriedly executing the last few duties required of the secretary of the Surrey club, leads me to believe that you have on the same attire that you sported while at the ground. Noticing that you have donned the Surrey tie, and are carrying a walking stick presented by the MCC, if the engraving is anything to go by, you need to have excellent reasons for the slightly worn pair of cufflinks bearing the coat of arms of the Free Imperial City of Hamburg that I find on your shirtsleeves. It certainly hints at cricketing connections."

Our famous visitor's smile overcame his slight embarrassment. "Vanity can be quite a cause for fluster. Yet, Mr Holmes, this does prove that I have come to the right man. Indeed in Hamburg I made the highest score in the game and was given a bat. Cuff links were presented to the entire team."

Charles Alcock looked at us and smiled courteously. "I understand I can trust you both to exercise discretion in a matter of extreme importance and, dare I say, not a little delicacy."

We nodded. Mr Alcock settled down on the sofa and held the cup of coffee my friend had offered him. "Mr Holmes, I have had the most flattering recommendations about you from Captain Henry Holden."

Holmes smiled. "In the light of what took place when our Australian friends went in to have lunch at Trent Bridge, surely you do not attach much weight to the captain's recommendations."

Mr Alcock laughed.

"Having had the assurance of your discretion, I will agree. I must say that I did not stop with Captain Holden's testimony — or Hellfire Jack as he is often called in careful whispers. Mr William Wright, the surveyor, a member of the Notts committee and a man for whom we have the highest regard, has also spoken of you in terms of the most eloquent praise for bringing to light the shady affair surrounding Selby."

I could not contain my surprise any longer.

"Holmes! Were you really involved in the investigations on the conduct of the English cricketers in the Colonies? I did not even know about it."

Mr Alcock laughed again, this time with more assurance. "I must say, Mr Holmes, that if there was any doubt I harboured about the degree of your discretion it has been dispelled."

Holmes looked at me over his linked fingers. "Yes, Watson. Earlier this year when I was away from London for a fortnight, I was engaged by the Nottinghamshire County Cricket Club to look into certain incidents that had gone on in the Antipodean summer. Unfortunately my findings did not reflect too well on John Selby, the professional cricketer."

Charles Alcock looked grave. "I can tell you in the greatest confidence gentlemen that Selby will never play for a representative England side again. However, in that case there is nothing that can be done to repair the damage. What we do need to do is to focus on the new problem here."

Holmes agreed. "I am sure you have plenty to tell, sir. Your telegram was dispatched at three and you have come here at half past seven, in spite of the encumbrances associated with the social part of the social game that is the lot of a club secretary. If I am not mistaken, you need our help regarding something that you fear may take place tomorrow. So, we are running against the clock. Please arrange your thoughts and let us know every detail of the matter."

Mr Alcock coughed. "With diplomatic relations under threat there is the problem that we cannot take the assistance of the police force. But I have been told that you can help even when the Yard is left without a clue. Mr Holmes, having dealt with the Nottinghamshire matter, you surely know that there are elements in the noble game that are less than desirable."

Holmes nodded, pausing for the slightest moment to cast a meaningful look at me.

"Indeed, bookmakers seem to be among the chief patrons of the game in the Colonies, almost as it was in England some sixty years ago," Charles Alcock continued. "This is but to be expected in a game where the line between gentlemen and professionals is almost invisible to the naked English eye. I will be the first one to say, Mr Holmes, that the Australians are wonderful cricketers, skilled enough to be our equals. However, as Shaw and Shrewsbury's tour has no doubt shown you, there are matters apart from just playing the game. The colonies do not possess the class of men from which our Hornbys, Webbes and Harrises are drawn, the class of gentlemen of leisure who can afford to give time and trouble to organising the pastime, and keeping up its moral and social tone. The Australian cricketers, you see, may not really consider themselves professionals, but they all make elaborate pecuniary speculations on their English tours. They pool their resources and float the tours as financial ventures. So, few of them can regard cricket in the disinterested English manner, financially speaking."

"All except Alick Banermann who comes at a fixed price, unaffected by the gates or the results."

"Perhaps, Mr Holmes, I'm sure you're right. I always say that cricket in the Colony is as amateur athletic sports and amateur rowing in England would be if university running and boating men added to their income by their strength and skill. The game is semi-professional, and incurs the scandals which are common in professional running and rowing, and which were common in the Ring, when there was a Ring. As we can see in the case of Ulyett and Selby, attempts to bribe English professionals to sell a match against very large sums is prevalent in the Colonies."

Holmes spoke as Mr Alcock stopped for breath, "Pardon me for interrupting such a stirring statement, Mr Alcock, but do you mean to say that bookmaking is limited in England? I can assure you it is not."

The Surrey secretary shook his head. "It is not that betting is not prevalent in our land, Mr Holmes. However, when you look into the amounts which recently made our professionals stray from the path at Melbourne, they were so large that we can safely say that all the bets made on all the English cricket for the whole year would not cover them. We can only rejoice that such blatant betting for large sums is unknown at home. The fact is probably that the Colonists have that provincial *esprit de corps* which only cares for the result of a match. One Colony, or one town, sets its heart on beating another, and all are excessively anxious to beat strangers. Consequently men bet highly on that which interests them deeply. At home we want to see good cricket, and are not overwhelmed by mortification when we lose, or puffed up with pride when we win. We play for play's sake far more than for victory."

"Your travels, I have ascertained, have taken you to Hamburg. Have you been up north to Yorkshire? Or west to where the famed WG Grace rules the cricket field, I believe, in Clifton?"

Charles Alcock looked first at Holmes and then at me and then burst out laughing.

"I appreciate your sense of humour, Mr Holmes. I daresay Peate, Emmett, Lockwood, Ulyett and the others play to win as much or even more than our Colonial friends. And in the shire of Graces, we can hardly expect the Champion to yield an inch. However, in the Doctor's case, bless his great heart, it is not so much the thought of financial interests, but the petulance of an overgrown schoolboy. As for the Yorkshire side, as you must know very well, the northern county team is almost entirely composed of professionals. No, my dear sir, I must say that I trust the Colonial vice will never take firm root at The Oval. Or at the Lord's."

Holmes sat there, linking his fingers, eyes closed in thought.

"I must say Mr Alcock, I am most impressed by your eloquence. I may have some scepticism about some of your convictions about the geographical and social seclusion of the bookmaking menace, and what you take for my sense of humour is actually spoken in earnest as a logical query; but I could hardly have expected a more telling speech even if faced with one who had come prepared with the entire idea scribbled down on notepaper."

For the second time in the evening, Mr Alcock looked a little embarrassed. "In that case let me confess, Mr Holmes, that those words were not entirely extempore. You may be aware that from the month of May this year, a new weekly periodical *Cricket – The Weekly Records of the Game* has been published. I happen to be the editor of this publication, and there was a piece on the Colonial vice that I myself wrote for the first issue. Most of what I have said had been prepared for the article."

"You are a remarkable man, Mr Alcock," I exclaimed. "How do you find the time required for all your activities, from the Football Association to the Surrey County Cricket Club to the magazine? I understand that you also edit the Lillywhite Annual."

As Mr Alcock bowed politely in response, Holmes remarked, "Perhaps that is one of the virtues of the gentleman of leisure Mr Alcock had been talking about."

"Indeed, Mr Holmes, but I should confess that the office of the Secretary of the Surrey County Club is a paid position, and I do draw a salary of £250 per annum and a £50 bonus."

"That may be, sir, but if you are convinced that the vice will never affect The Oval what makes you come to me on the evening of a great match?"

Charles Alcock leaned forward with his arms stretched outwards. "Regardless of the faith I have in the English spirit of cricket and the gentleman cricketer, it is part of my duties as the secretary of the Surrey Cricket Club to exercise vigilance to my fullest capability. I have reason to believe that dirty business is being contemplated, and the evil hand of betting, involving large sums of money, is preparing to strike at the ground tomorrow. I am sure that the foundations of the Club are strong enough to withstand such strikes, but it may be opportune to nip the villainy in the bud. However, before going into the specific details, I must insist once again that this should be treated with utmost discretion. You see, the Australian press, and that includes one of the players in their side named Tom Horan, would be very likely to respond in kind to the criticism over the Melbourne incident that they received from the press of this country."

"Of course."

"Besides, there are as well other internal forces within the country, which may make the Surrey County Cricket Club susceptible to an angry backlash. The Lancashire committee is not at all pleased with our selection of Maurice Read ahead of their Crossland, and neither is their press. *The Manchester Guardian* is harping on the better man being left out of the side. Yet, Dr Watson will perhaps agree, we were left with no choice in the matter. Crossland throws. His action is unclean. The Australians have already made a fuss after facing Mycroft ..."

"I beg your pardon. Facing whom?" Sherlock Holmes asked in sudden surprise.

"William Mycroft of Derbyshire."

"Ah," my friend expelled a sigh with some apparent sign of relief.

"The lad does have a distinct jerk while delivering, and ever since Joseph Frank broke Spoff's finger in the summer of 1880 and they lost the last Oval match while The Demon sat out with a bandaged hand, the Colonials have been very sensitive about bowlers of questionable actions. So, there was no way we could allow Crossland in the team. But, the Lancashire men have painted the exclusion with a local tint. Any sign of mismanagement on our part will lead to fierce criticism."

"And you do not attribute this attitude of the folks of our own Northern county as the same provincial *esprit de corps* which makes the Colonials want to win?"

Charles Alcock looked up, rather confused, entrapped by the logical serpent of a question. Holmes changed the subject without pressing further.

"But, sir, what is it that makes you think there may be sinister bookmaking at work tomorrow?"

The gentleman put his hand inside the breast pocket of his coat and produced a plain white envelope.

CHAPTER 3

THE WARNING

"THIS WAS delivered to me in the pavilion today. It was just as the two teams had come in for lunch." Mr Alcock paused for thought and decided to add, "Actually I must be more specific. This envelope was left on a table in the committee room of the pavilion, with my name on it. There is no postmark. It was actually Hornby himself who attracted my attention to it. Naturally I opened it and then got the shock of my life."

I drew my chair closer to the one in which Sherlock Holmes sat. The envelope was otherwise unmarked. "Mr Charles Alcock, Surrey County Cricket Club" was printed on it with carefully crafted letters. Holmes put his long, thin fingers inside the envelope and drew out a note. On a single, unevenly torn piece of paper was written the following message in a rather careless hand: "Increase security on second day. Heavy betting. Or Melbourne may be repeated."

Holmes held the piece of paper against the lamp, looked at it from different angles, ran his fingers lightly over it and finally, bringing it up close to his nose, even sniffed at it.

"If it found its way into the pavilion, it was obviously left by someone from the Club or one of the members of the two teams."

"Yes, Mr Holmes, and I cannot ask anyone about it without exposing ourselves to the worst scandal. The Australians are our guests, we cannot accuse them or make them apprehensive about the possible ugliness of events to come. We as the cradle of the game are expected to set the moral standards by which cricket is played. And as I said, the Australian press would soon be up in arms. There are so many different eggshells, many of them diplomatic, which one has to avoid treading on when such great matches are organised. The Lancashire press and committee, as I already told you, have not been our foremost supporters because of Crossland. Also, the Champion is not entirely enamoured of us at the current moment."

"And what has Surrey done to incur the wrath of Dr Grace?"

Mr Alcock looked rather embarrassed as he proceeded with a hasty explanation.

"It was actually in some ways my own fault, allowing a particular piece in the periodical I spoke about. One of our writers, under the pseudonym *Pavilion Gossip*, wrote an article to the effect that during the match against Australia at Chichester, the United Eleven led by WG fielded so loosely that the team could be called Untied. It was terrible wordplay, but made with the lightest of hearts. But WG had recently suffered from mumps and the spirit is often testy when a sportsman goes through the lengthy process of recuperation. He did not take it very well. As editor of the publication, I have to absorb some of the bitterness."

Holmes was still absorbed by the piece of paper.

"As the players ate, and I read the note, I looked at the crowd. It was so great that despite the efforts of the police and the stewards, the spectators kept encroaching onto the field. You see, after the representative match of the summer of '80 we received complaints that our facilities were not good enough for the patrons. Hence, for the last couple of years we have made the ground more suitable for the paying public to enjoy the entertainment. New stands, both covered and terraced, have been constructed for the spectators. Seats have also been provided around the ground. There have been facilities erected for the press and the printing of scorecards. The western stands have been enlarged and there is a refurbished wooden annex to the east end of the pavilion. Mr Trotman and Mr Tunewall, and the traders Ind Coope and Company, sell refreshments around the ground. The earth that was excavated for the enclosure of the Vauxhall Creek has been used to create a circle of embankments around the ground, so the standing spectators have a much better view. You see, gentlemen, we have taken every measure to make The Oval a first-rate ground for sporting events, and it attracts people."

"Yes sir," I agreed enthusiastically. "I was there today and I know what an admirable ground it has become. The crowd swelled to somewhere in the regions of 20,000 I should say."

"Indeed, Dr Watson. But, great as it is for the finances of the club and for the pleasure of those viewing sports, the vast numbers have meant that we could not maintain the boundary of the playing area as planned. The hundreds who had stood behind seven or eight rows in those parts of the ground that do not yet have a stand now grew bold and squatted on the grass during the luncheon interval. They remained there even after play resumed. With the Australian wickets falling so regularly, the interest showed no sign of ebbing. The grandstand and the terrace were sold out. Sometimes, a ball was driven towards the folk inside the boundary and they jumped out of the way. The fielders were faced with the trouble of running around the spectators as well as after the ball. The strokes that could have been restricted to three runs became fours. I dare say we as England benefitted quite a bit more than our guests since it was our batsmen who batted for most of the day after the luncheon. As the Secretary of the Club, I am supposed to use my discretion and judgement; I am responsible for matches taking place without any hitch. I wondered how, in such a great crowd, I would be able to ensure enough vigilance that no villainous element could make his way in. Involving the police would lead to all sorts of diplomatic and public relations difficulties. That is when I was advised to approach you."

Holmes now took the envelope itself, held it up to the light, and very carefully studied both the exterior and the flap.

"I find your account of singular interest, Mr Alcock. Here Watson, take a look at this sheet. There is a diligent Scottish doctor in a hospital on the far eastern shores of Japan who wrote a paper published in *Nature* two years ago.

If it had been acted upon with rather more energy than the authorities and the scientific community have shown till now, it could have possibly led us to the identification of the sender from this exhibit itself. There are smudges from a thumb which I see all over the sheet, and if Dr Faulds is right, which I have every reason to believe he is, the identity of the individual could have been uniquely determined by the distinctive whorls of the thumb impressions. However, since science will keep us waiting for what I surmise will be a decade or two, let us carry on along an alternate route of deduction."

I looked at the note carefully, trying to exercise my mental faculties following the footsteps of my friend.

"Several of the letters seem to be written over twice or thrice."

"Exactly, Watson. That tells us that whoever sent this took considerable pains to disguise his normal hand. The characters are printed in a way to resemble the standard way of writing, eliminating any semblance of a personal longhand style. Wherever there was some characteristic flourish, it has been hidden by careful scribbles of the pen. Yet, from the strokes of the pen, I can tell with certainty that the writing and the overwriting has been made by one and the same man. The blotting paper has been used but carelessly, I would say deliberately so. Which would imply, my dear sir, that his writing would in normal circumstances be very familiar to you."

The Surrey Secretary looked both enthralled by the deduction and thoughtful at the implications. "There are so many of those with access to the pavilion who have communicated with me in writing. But, Mr Holmes, can you really say all that from the writing itself?"

"Handwriting examination is, I believe, still in its germinal phase as a device of detection, Mr Alcock. From a free flowing hand, it is possible to tell the gender, degree of education, state of mind and even shades of the character of the writer. In this case we cannot go that far because of the obvious self-tampering that has taken place. But there are other things that can be divined."

I looked long and hard at the piece of paper that he held in his hand. "It seems to have been hastily torn out of a notepad or a notebook."

Holmes smiled. "Yes, Watson, the irregular tear does give that impression of haste. Yet, the unevenness of the tear does not show any continuous stretch at the edges, contradicting the hypothesis of a quick tear. There is a concave rip at the top, followed by a somewhat straighter tear to the left and again another concave scoop to the bottom of the left edge. These three patterns seem to be three separate endeavours at tearing off the piece of paper. And if you notice, the right and the bottom edges of the sheet are perfectly straight. What does that suggest?"

"The writer tore it off by pulling downward and rightward?"

"I hardly think it was a clean jerk, Watson. He carefully tore off part of the top, went through with the removal and then scooped out a part to the left."

Charles Alcock spoke now with a great deal of excitement, "He deliberately removed something written on the top and to the left."

"Exactly, my dear sir. Something written, printed or embossed. And if you feel the piece of paper, it is thicker and more expensive than what can be found in a regular notebook. The writer was worried that you could have got some indication of his identity, even after his disguising his writing, if the top or right side remained visible."

"Letterhead," I exclaimed.

"Excellent Watson," Holmes cried. "The weight and texture of the paper along with the carefully removed parts hint that it is the stationery of a hotel."

"Brilliant Mr Holmes, simply brilliant," Mr Alcock's calm features gleamed with enthusiasm. "We can easily ascertain whether or not it is from the Tavistock …"

"Why do you think it is the Tavistock?"

"Why, sir, the Australians are putting up there. They have taken a liking to the establishment since the summer of '80."

"I see, Mr Alcock, you are quite certain that the letter was sent by one of the Colonial visitors, no doubt based on the theory of the proliferation of bookmaking in their part of the world of which you have spoken. Yet, we must not be hasty in eliminating any other possibility. Perhaps the only group we can exclude is our own professional cricketers in the team. That, to my great relief, eliminates the involvement of Ulyett, at least from taking responsibility for this communication. I understand you have separate facilities for the lunch of the professional cricketers."

"Why of course, Mr Holmes, we take every care to preserve the pavilion for the gentlemen and have separate changing rooms for the players. The Colonials, due to the obscure definition of the categories in their case, and given that they are our guests, have been extended the facilities of the pavilion."

"Except in Trent Bridge where the eminent Captain Holden still cracks the whip with his iron hand."

Mr Alcock coughed apologetically and spoke gravely. "That was an unfortunate incident, Mr Holmes, and I can assure you none of the other grounds, big or small, will make the same mistake. However, while we can exclude men like Peate and Ulyett, we cannot yet be sure of the identity of the gentleman who sent me this missive, or what dreadful dangers stare at us as we take field tomorrow. I am at a loss how to prevent any dubious underhand dealing without giving rise to scandal of the worst kind."

Sherlock Holmes put his fingers together and looked at the ceiling. "I shall glance into the case for you and I have no doubt that we shall reach some definite result. Let the weight of the matter rest upon me now, and do not let your mind dwell upon it any further. The greatest danger that you should be dealing with, if I have paid sufficient heed to the words of Watson here, is the deviousness of Fred Spofforth when England bat again."

Mr Alcock winced with genuine feeling. "Yes, Mr Holmes. The very look in his eye, with his Mephistophelean moustache on that lean face, gives me the shivers."

I nodded in keen agreement. "The Demon, as he is called. He destroyed MCC at Lord's in 1878, and it was distinctly fortuitous for our men that he broke his finger prior to the match in 1880. As far as I remember he did the hat-trick against Lord Harris's side when they visited the Colonies."

Yet, our engaging discussion notwithstanding, Holmes was not to be diverted into the cricketing talk. "What I require from you, Mr Alcock, is a detailed itinerary of the Australian cricketers for the entire visit, including the places where they have stayed. The same goes for the members of the representative England side assembled for this match, if I could have the whereabouts of their lodging and travel during the days of the match and the days leading up to it."

"Why, certainly Mr Holmes. I have most of the details with me. I brought them along in anticipation of your demands. I will write down whatever additional details you desire that may not have been included in the documents."

"That was most sensible of you, Mr Alcock, I wish every client thought as far ahead as you do. Apart from that we need to be able to get into The Oval tomorrow before the match commences without queuing up for the public tickets which can be purchased for five shillings. Watson, I believe, has made the arrangements to be there to watch the cricketers on the second day, but I have no such means of entry."

"Of course, sir, here are two passes for you that will get you access to the ground. Present these at the entrance to the pavilion and you will be ushered up to the Member's quarters."

At this point in the narrative I will confess that I was more than glad when the esteemed gentleman took his leave of us after a couple of minutes. The very thought of being able to watch the proceedings of the following day from the famed pavilion of the great ground brought forth a warm glow of happiness inside me that I feared was shining on my visage as would befit an adolescent boy given the chance to meet his cricketing heroes. Apprehensive of demonstrating my boundless joy at being able to watch the game from such a position of privilege, even when rather more sinister events were afoot, it was with distinct relief that I saw Mr Alcock out.

Yet, I have no doubt he of all men would have understood the fascination for the great game that keeps the flame of the child burning within the man even as the years go by fast enough to blow out the many lively candles of young dreams.

CHAPTER 4

THE NOBLE AND THE IGNOBLE

THE ANTICIPATION of the morrow was mingled in my mind with a thousand unanswered questions. During the events of the *Study in Scarlet*, and after that, I have had occasion to observe at close proximity the way my friend puts his singular mind to solving problems that puzzled many of the high-ranking members of the police force. It pained me that I had been in the dark about his involvement in the unravelling of the web of devious acts of which our cricketers had been accused in the Antipodean lands, events that had created quite a sensation in the press during the spring.

I dearly wanted to ask him about Midwinter's accusation, Shaw's enquiry, the roles of Selby and Ulyett. However, when I cast my eyes at him, Holmes was already silent and deeply engrossed in thought. His fingertips were still pressed together in habitual manner, legs stretched out in front of him, gaze directed upward towards the ceiling. After a while he took down from the rack the old and oily clay pipe, which perhaps to him was a counsellor, and, having lit it, leaned back in his chair, with the thick blue cloud-wreaths spinning up from him, a look of infinite concentration in his face.

Assuming that he would not want to be disturbed, I busied myself in preparation for an early night. As I was on the verge of retiring to my room, Holmes opened his eyes and exclaimed, "It's a pity, Watson, that the great Charles Darwin has left us recently."

The great scientist and the author of that incredible work *The Voyage of the Beagle* had indeed passed away in the month of April that year, but I could not but wonder what connection the theory of evolution could have with the current problem concerning cricket and bookmaking. Holmes laughed as he detected my surprise.

"Great minds leave a residual usefulness in areas far removed from their direct sphere of expertise, Watson. I spoke of Dr Henry Faulds of Tokyo who has done such magnificent work on fingerprinting. According to his final correspondence with me, coming across the unscientific objections of our dim-witted police force, Faulds had sent his views to Mr Darwin. I am not sure the old man was able to do much with it, but if he has aroused enough interest in the scientific community something worthwhile may well come out of it. But the reason why I mentioned Darwin now is quite different. It was his belief that insects and plants co-evolve and are interdependent, and he held this belief to his dying day."

"You amaze me, Holmes," I said. "This degree of knowledge of the theory of evolution is in direct contrast to your own theory of facts being akin to furniture in the brain, and a greater accumulation of them leading to displacement of some to the lumber room."

"What are we, Watson, even the most rational among us, but masses of contradiction? Let me loose in a Valley of Fear and I will vouch that 'All knowledge comes useful to the detective.' I have not studied the intricacies of Darwin's theory, but I profess to the same line of thought in that society and crime, linked by their mutual fascination for money, co-evolve and are interdependent. This is what leads to my serious disagreement with our dear Mr Charles Alcock who thinks stolid British morality will prevent the tentacles of betting and match manipulation from spreading across Lord's and The Oval."

"You think the amateur England cricketer is susceptible to the vice of making money from betting on cricket?"

"Why not, Watson? The amateur England cricketer often makes many times more money from the game than the most highly paid professional. The difference is that he puts it down as expenses. During the case that I worked on for the Nottinghamshire County Cricket Club, there were many professional cricketers who complained of this and I did come across plenty of evidence for the claim. Do you know how much our own Champion made when he toured the Australian parts in 1873? It was a figure that would knock you back with astonishment. Aside from that, money is a necessity for everyone, gentleman or player. It is the degree that is different. With huge sums casting an ominous shadow, every great name and rank can be made to look murky. And if high enough stakes were offered to unsettle the balance of our professionals in Australia, the same can be done here in England. With so much interest in the game, it is not too difficult to imagine."

"You are saying that amateur cricketers cannot be excluded from the suspicions."

"My dear Watson, we cannot exclude anyone from suspicion. When our Mr Alcock said that the stakes on the game are not great enough here, he was recounting not what was fact but what he dearly wanted to be fact. Despite his obvious astuteness, he has fallen prey to this very human failing. During the Nottinghamshire revelation I did point out that as far back as 1751 a match between Old Etonians and an England XI featured a wager of £1,500 in addition to side bets totalling £20,000. Land and property were also staked. The same class of landed gentry, who passed the laws dealing with crimes against property such as poaching and squatting, prepared the laws of cricket."

"Holmes, I thought you were not interested in the game."

"I am not interested in the contrived battle between the bat and the ball and the outcome, Watson, but the periphery of the supposedly noble game is embroidered with a strand of tarnished gold. In 1794, the Earls of Winchilsea and Darnley wagered 1,000 guineas on a match between their respective sides. You see, moneyed gentlemen of leisure have had a long history of staking huge sums on the game. If such great amounts are played for, can you expect the matches to be free from the occasional result being poked and prodded past the desired threshold for the sake of profits?"

"Holmes, to me till this moment cricket was a pristine game. You have successfully managed, using a cricketing expression, to queer the pitch for me."

"Now that you know it, Watson, you will do well not to forget it in a hurry. You expressed surprise when I demonstrated eagerness to forget which of sun, moon or earth revolved around which of the other. Let me tell you that the sports fan, who develops his *weltanschauung* based on his fascination with the romance of the game, shows supreme alacrity in forgetting the facts that jar with his view of the sporting world. In the Hambledon matches, that supposed cradle of cricket, about which our Nyren is so eloquent, £500 a side was the normal wager. Those who devour *The Young Cricketer's Tutor* with a devoted soul would like to believe the cricketers of the past were nothing short of angels. Tell the old timers today that Alfred Mynn was once hissed at in the Maidstone Market because of his supposed hand in fixing a match. Now the very ones who hissed on that day may deny it most vehemently, intent on manufacturing a belief that the great days of their youth had been golden ones."

"It is most interesting, Holmes, that you used a German term in relation to cricket, given that the game is as yet unpopular on the continent. What's more, Mr Charles Alcock mentioned playing the game in Hamburg. That makes it quite a remarkable coincidence."

"Indeed? What would you say, Watson, if I told you that the first detailed guide to the game was drawn up not in England, but in the Bavarian village of Schnepfental? This was in 1796, the work of a teacher named Johann

Christian Friedrich Gutsmuths. This document called cricket 'a magnificent game which lends itself to being played even without money. As a game for money it is greatly preferable to cards.'"

I raised my hands in a plea of resignation. "Stop, Holmes. I have been granted the opportunity of watching what should be a most engrossing game of cricket, which I hope will end in a famous victory for England, from the hallowed confines of the Oval pavilion. You have an inclination to drain the last bit of fascination I yet harbour for the game. Please desist!"

Holmes laughed with good humour as he got up from his armchair.

"It saves me from ennui, Watson. My life is spent in one long effort to escape the commonplaces of existence, and there is hardly anything more commonplace than taking an ideal view of sports and games. But I will leave you to get some sleep, if The Demon in your thoughts allows you. I will be up and about early tomorrow morning, but will return in good time for us to start for The Oval. I will undertake that you will not miss a moment of the game that is so precious to you. I, on the other hand, have to find out exactly how precious it is about to get."

CHAPTER 5

THE RIDE THROUGH TIME

TRUE TO his word, Holmes had already left when I awoke the following morning. The famous, fateful day of 29th August, 1882, had dawned gloomy, my fear of rain intensified by the promised view from the pavilion. As I breakfasted alone, the skies grew darker and darker till at half past nine the first drops of rain could be contained no longer.

There was no sign of Holmes as I sat ready to depart despite the murky weather. I would be less than honest if I forgot to mention that a couple of uncharitable thoughts did cross my mind as I considered the possibility of my friend delaying his return. The match was scheduled to resume at half past eleven and I looked forward to catching every moment of it from the windows of the pavilion.

In want of something to do while waiting, I picked up the *Times* and turned to the report of the previous day's play. I was surprised to find the harsh words it employed about Ulyett — "A little too venturesome". On opening the

Daily Telegraph, the tone was hardly any different with an unflattering description of how he "would persist in running out at dangerous deliveries, and in the end in following these tactics he missed Spofforth and had his bails whipped off by Blackham." It was rather unwarranted that the sterling all-rounder was criticised even after scoring 26, which was the highest managed by any of our batsmen by some distance. Besides, to my untrained eyes, his adventurous methods had actually got him the runs. We cannot ignore the fact that he came in to bat after the Champion had fallen and then we had lost Barlow almost immediately afterwards. Lucas was the other extreme, but one wondered how profitable such measures were, seeing that he had batted 10 more minutes than Ulyett, faced five more balls and scored just 9. The only man who made a contribution of comparable proportions was the local player Maurice Read, and he too opted for the way of the sword even as the light grew wretched.

As I read the reports, the clock ticked past ten and the rainfall increased to a downpour. There was still no sign of my friend. Impatiently I paced about the room, looking frequently at the rain drops drumming against the window, willing the sun to shine. It was a quarter past the hour when I heard his steps on the stairs and Holmes entered cheerily, with none of the blackness that prevailed outside. He was in his overcoat and deerstalker, a smile spread across his face.

"Watson, come on. The hansom waits at the door. We have no time to lose. To get to the Surrey side of London in this weather is no mean task."

Grabbing my hat and walking stick I rushed down the stairs like a child eager for a treat. To assuage my own fears I asked, "But, Holmes, will the rain clear up?"

"That is not within my powers to foretell, Watson. What I can tell you is that in spite of the weather there promises to be even more spectators in the ground than there were yesterday. By all indications they already sit there, in a belt, on the uncovered grass around the ground, protected by their umbrellas, macintoshes and coats. All for the love of a sport which I find rather ridiculous."

Rain lashed heavily against the windows of the cab as we set off.

The journey was long, making for the other side of the Thames. The congestion of the London streets and the incessant rain did enough to slow our progress. There were times I wished that the game had been arranged in nearby St John's Wood. If the MCC were a little more accommodating in recognising Colonial talent, representative matches could be held at Lord's, within a short walk of our Baker Street lodgings. However, would an MCC Secretary have extended invitation to non-members to watch the game from the famous Long Room? It seemed to me infinitely more prudent to count my blessings.

The hour-long drive allowed me to ask my friend about his morning excursions. Holmes was emphatic in his reply, "Most fruitful, Watson, most fruitful. My journey to the Tavistock Hotel was discouraging. The stationery the establishment uses is not similar to the torn sheet of paper received by our client. Neither did I find a match at the different lodgings the English cricketers have been using.

But the details so kindly given by Mr Charles Alcock last night did help me track down the origin of the paper. That, in turn, gives some more insight into the problem."

"So, where was the letter written?"

"The Australian cricketers prefer to practise at the grounds kept at Mitcham Green by the professional cricketer James Southerton. It is a public house with an adjacent wicket; the cricketers seem extremely fond of the roast beef and the foaming tankards of bitter available after their exercise. It was there that I found the matching stationery, kept on the bar counter in case some enterprising customer wants to mix his ale with a spot of letter writing."

"Holmes," I cried. "If the letter was delivered yesterday, in such a hurried manner, it must have been written yesterday as well. Else there would be no pressing necessity to use that flimsy stationery, especially if one had the luxury of framing it overnight."

"You reason extremely well, Watson. I must say your methods of deduction have been coming along most splendidly."

"But, Holmes, it makes no sense. It is a long way to Mitcham Green from the Tavistock and then back to the hotel or to the ground. The Australian cricketers were at The Oval yesterday. Surely none of them would have gone so far to practise on the day of the match, especially since it was raining yesterday morning as well."

"As I have said often, Watson, if we have eliminated the impossible, whatever remains, however improbable, must be the truth."

"You mean the Australians were crazy enough to go all the way to Mitcham to have a hit yesterday morning?"

"You do an excellent group of men grave injustice, Watson. Most of them were reasonable enough to make for the ground in their hansom cabs straight from the hotel. But some of them do have a bit more of the demonic about them."

There was a twinkle in his eye as he made this devilish allusion, and I could not hide my excitement.

"Spofforth went there to work on his bowling?"

"I have it from the helping hands of the establishment that he did. Apparently, the Australians are taking this match extremely seriously, and some of them are complaining of getting stale after so many days on the tour. It induced Spofforth to start practising ahead of the match, and some believe it is the first time in his life that he has done anything of that sort. But the mind of a great practitioner, set upon some aspect of his art, may have a compulsion to work on till perfection is attained. It seems he was adamant in carrying on with some experiment that he was making in the process of developing his deliveries."

"Holmes, you mean Spofforth himself wrote this letter?"

"It is a capital mistake to theorise in advance of the facts, Watson. I have told you Spofforth was there. But there could have been other men. Indeed, it would be rather careless for the management of the Australian side to let a player of such importance and eccentricity as Spofforth wander unattended on the morning of the match. Two men from the team's management travelled with him. They sat in the bar as the bowler toiled at the wicket, helped in his efforts by some young local lads and another

Australian cricketer not taking part in the match, by the name of Percy McDonnell. Unfortunately, the officials accompanying him were in no way as recognisable as the demon bowler himself. Hence, they were not really noticed by those running the establishment."

"But surely now we can be positive that the letter came from the Australian camp?"

"Indeed. All evidence points to it." My companion looked out of the cab window with a satisfied air. "The weather seems to be clearing, Watson, and soon we may have a game on our hands, as well as the one that's already afoot."

It was gratifying, indeed, but my head was still in a whirl with all the new information. "If the letter was written in a hurry at the public house in Mitcham Green, surely something must have taken place during the visit."

"You sum it up most succinctly and well," Holmes said, looking rather pleased. "There are still many obscure aspects, but we have been able to narrow down the identity of the letter-writer to within a known set of people. The difficulty that does arise, however, is that we cannot mention the letter openly to the Australian team, because of the stipulation of secrecy imposed upon us by our client. Yet, there is a tiny beam of light which in all probability may lead us to the truth. The excursions to the Tavistock Hotel and Southerton's have not been the whole extent of my adventures this morning. As a doctor you need to test the pulse or listen to the heart of the patient to gauge the extent of his illness. The same holds true for me as a consulting detective. I have to isolate the affected part of this great city and look, listen and feel for the signs and symptoms of malfunction. Several street bookmakers are busy at work in backyards of some terraced houses, their 'dogger-outs' ever vigilant with their elaborate set of signals to alert these industrious workers in case of an approaching member of the police force."

"You think there is a connection to the warning received by Charles Alcock yesterday?"

"It is a mistake to theorize before one has the full data, Watson. Insensibly one begins to twist facts to suit theories, instead of the other way around. I will have to study the activity on the ground, then put the pieces together to form my conclusions."

We were nearing the Vauxhall Bridge and the rain had finally stopped. I was not hopeful of a timely start, but it did look likely that play would commence not long after the scheduled hour. Looking out of the window, I noticed how the weather had changed into a rather unseasonal bitter cold. Men were drawing their overcoats closely around them. It did indeed look a blessing to have been invited to witness the game from the warmth of the pavilion.

With still some way to go till we reached the ground, I touched upon a matter which had been plaguing me from the previous evening.

"Holmes, now that I have been put abreast of your involvement with the Nottinghamshire committee, could you tell me what exactly went on with our cricketers during their last visit to the Colonies?"

My friend looked genuinely surprised. "Surely, Watson, you have read plenty of reports of the incidents. Even Mr

Alcock's periodical, I am given to understand, covered the facts in some detail."

"They do hint at what happened, the various allegations and rebuttals, but the specifics are rendered confusing by sketchy and often contradictory details."

Holmes was showing a strong inclination to curl himself up on his seat, eyes closed and the black clay pipe thrusting out like the bill of a strange bird. I came to the conclusion that he was absorbed in contemplation of the events. Having gone through his account with me a number of times after the present affair of The Oval had ended, and having laid my hands on a good deal of literature on the topic, for a moment I will ask leave to remove my own insignificant personality and to describe events which occurred at Melbourne in the December of '81.

Alfred Shaw, the Nottinghamshire professional, had taken his band of men on this tour of the Antipodes. The initial days had been quite successful with the strong England side triumphing over a couple of weaker country teams, playing odds matches and beating a strong New South Wales side by 68 runs. After this they prepared themselves to face a star-studded Victorian side at Melbourne. What went on in this game can hardly be described as anything short of scandalous.

Hordes of people flocked to watch the important match. Shaw later recounted that as many as 20,000 turned up for the second day. The local supporters were a happy lot as play began. Opener Percy McDonnell batted well as did the prince of wicketkeepers, the bearded Jack Blackham. In spite of Yorkshireman Ted Peate's accurate spinners, the home team notched up an impressive 251.

By the middle of the second day, Joey Palmer and Frank Allan, excellent bowlers both, had made the ball cut viciously off the pitch to bowl Shaw's team out for 146. The follow-on rule in operation at that time ensured that the Englishmen had to bat again immediately. By the time play ended on the second evening Alfred Shaw's side had lost two wickets and were still plenty in arrears.

The following morning saw a fightback of great spirit by the young Nottinghamshire batsman of exceptional potential called Arthur Shrewsbury. His serene half century, followed by a storm, ensured that the match remained undecided when the stumps were drawn at the end of the third day. Shaw's side were on 167 for 7.

Shaw's men were due to set sail for Adelaide at one in the morning. However, the Victorians were extremely eager to finish the game, ostensibly because they believed they had the upper hand. Shaw consulted the team's touring manager James Lillywhite and the two Englishmen wisely decided that the best thing to do was to leave the course of action to the Victorians.

In the course of later investigation, much of it carried out by my friend, it was revealed that enormous amounts of money had been bet on a victory for the home side. One of the participating players confided to Holmes, "The bookmakers were standing up, doing business as if they were in Tattersall's Ring." Some documents later brought to light that the bookmakers had paid the steamship company £300 to delay its departure.

The next day, Shaw was greatly surprised to hear that the bookmakers were offering odds of 30 to 1 against the

Englishmen, and was reportedly aghast at what was going on. "Most extravagant odds were offered on the Victorian team, in spite of the fact that the weather was wet, and there was a possibility of the home batsmen having to play on a sticky wicket, to which they were unaccustomed," he related to Holmes during the investigations. It was the curious cricketer Billy Midwinter who reported the odds to him. I say curious because of the many peculiarities associated with Midwinter's cricket career. He had played for both Australia and England and had been the centre of controversy when, about to appear for Australia against Middlesex at Lord's, he was supposedly kidnapped by WG Grace who wanted him to play for Gloucestershire against Surrey at The Oval.

Now, to come back to the Melbourne match, his captain Shaw decided that he was prepared to bet a pound at such terms. All the members of the England side bet a pound apiece on their win.

When the weather relented and play could be resumed, the wicket resembled a proper mud pudding. Shrewsbury continued to bat magnificently to remain unbeaten on 80, and the England innings came to an end at 198. This left Victoria 94 to win, a target which looked simple enough but was not without its challenges on the treacherous turf.

As far as the game was concerned it was set up for an exciting finish, but the dark hand of manipulation was raising itself. Midwinter approached Shaw again with his next piece of information, which shook the captain to the core. According to the cricketer, Yorkshire's famed all-rounder Ulyett and Nottinghamshire's John Selby had been promised a bet of '£100 to nothing' on a Victorian win. The next part of Midwinter's missive sounded even more sinister. He claimed that the two professionals had approached him to participate in a 'fix'. Apparently another Nottinghamshire man, William Scotton, was also already involved in the ugly affair.

A surprised Shaw did not believe the cricketer at first, but soon events on the field unfolded in a manner to change his course of thought. Some of the antics looked definitely rigged. The captain confided to Holmes that certain Englishmen kept dropping chances, and one catch was taken by pure accident. "A remarkably curious circumstance was that after one ridiculously easy catch had been dropped, a batsman was out by the ball going up inside the fieldsman's arm and sticking there — not, I have reason to think, with the catcher's intentional aid." This was ascertained by my friend to be the catch of Harry Boyle, taken by Selby when the batsman had scored 43.

To his infinite credit, Shaw thwarted the intentions of the 'fixers' by marshalling his resources with canny captaincy. He denied the ball to both Midwinter and Ulyett, encouraged the trusted Ted Peate to keep bowling, and on that wet wicket the left-armer's deliveries spat up as they turned away. Apart from Boyle, only Palmer reached double figures.

In spite of the dropped catches, the wickets continued to fall. In the end, when Dick Barlow bowled Allan to end the match, the Victorians were still 18 runs short of the total managed by the men from England. An elated Shaw remarked with passion: "Whatever the scheme actually was, it failed."

The captain did indeed have his reasons to be pleased. All his men had staked a pound at enormous odds. Besides, as they boarded the ship, an expatriate Briton by the name of Sam Grimwood came over to meet them. This Halifax-born man had bet so heavily on Shaw's team that he had amassed a huge fortune because of the surprise result. The happy gambler Grimwood handed every member of Shaw's team a £10 note.

Yet, in spite of pecuniary gains, there was discontent in the side. Later Shaw revealed that Midwinter was ill-treated by some of the team because he had complained about the incident to his captain.

The captain, for his part, did proceed with an enquiry, but perhaps his happiness at the win in both cricket and cash made him temper his investigations. There was no concrete evidence of any underhand dealings and the allegations were dismissed. Shaw also lavished praise on Ulyett's undoubted proficiency on the cricket field and his ebullient character away from the game.

Yet, as the English cricketers returned to their native shores, the controversy was given a new lease of life. The *Australasian* continued to paint our cricketers in questionable colours. In the month of April, letters were sent to the cricket committees of Nottinghamshire and Yorkshire, with complaints about Selby and Ulyett respectively. At this juncture my friend was summoned to Trent Bridge to look into the matter. The men at Bramall Lane, with their strong Yorkshire sentiment against hiring external help, relied on the able resources of Sergeant Cuff.

Much of what these two extraordinary investigators unearthed has not been disclosed to the public. In the end Selby's character seemed more compromised than that of Ulyett or Scotton.

To men who love the sweet sound of the willow on leather, the smell of freshly cut grass, and delight in watching the men in white play this wonderful game on lush green fields, such dark disclosures can be unsettling and can test their love for the game to the utmost.

Yet, the inkling that all was not as it seemed in the world of cricket scarcely kept me from indulging in a glow of delight as we alighted in front of the pavilion building.

CHAPTER 6

INSIDE THE PAVILION

AMONG those thumbing through this sensational story more than a century after the events, many will perhaps picture us walking into the famous Long Room of the pavilion. It was not so. The new pavilion would not be built until thirteen years later; I remember that distinctly because it was the summer when the Champion, in his 47th year, batted as if rejuvenated by a relentless flow of life's unstoppable energy.

Nevertheless, on that day of late August, 1882, we were ushered into an imposing club room with magnificent oil paintings hanging on the walls and big windows through which we could see the sunlight starting to appear. At the entrance we passed the marble slab commemorating the great deeds of the Surrey side during the season of 1853, when they were unbeaten all summer, with victories over Sussex, Nottinghamshire and England. Mr Alcock met us with a visible sign of relief, introducing us simply as his guests of honour, showing us to our seats.

The moment brought with it both happiness and awe. Ushered into the comfortable wooden chair, I noticed seated not far away the famous figure of Lord Harris. Here was the erstwhile England captain, the great man of Kent cricket, and one who for all practical purposes ran the game in the country. He was in intense discussion with three other dignified gentlemen, whom I later ascertained to be the brothers Isaac and Vyell Walker of Middlesex and Frederick Burbidge of Surrey. The four together had been entrusted with the most difficult task of selecting the England side for this great match played in the South of England. All around the room variously stood and sat famous gentlemen associated with cricket whether as players, administrators or important patrons. In the far corner of the room I could see the magnificently moustachioed EM Grace, elder brother of the Champion and a most brilliant cricketer in his own right.

Looking out of the window, I was greeted by a fascinating sight. The clouds had parted and the sun was now peeping through. The patches of blue above were welcome for cricket-thirsty eyes. The scene below was one of cheerful confusion. The spectators attending seemed to be even more numerous than they had been on the day before. Most of them were respectable Londoners, although here and there a cluster of the rougher element could be glimpsed. As long as the game kept them from mischief, I had no objection to their presence. As my eyes moved around the ground, I noticed a few ladies had come out, braving the weather and toil, to witness the game. Interestingly, there were a fair number of men of the cloth, perhaps the many perpetual long-stops to be seen across the village greens around the counties.

The crowd were spilling out of every vantage point whence the game could be seen. There were even men creeping under the terraced stands, trying to find a way to view the proceedings from whatever crevice or crack provided an unblocked view. Some who had to stand behind rows of onlookers had been wise enough to arm themselves with stools, and now stood on them, creating a layer of fascinated eyes that looked over the heads of the people immediately in front. The gasworks overlooking the ground were dotted with intrepid climbers. The neighbouring public house had opened its roof, whether willing or not I am uncertain, and spectators had climbed out of the windows eager to watch the day's play.

The only sight that jarred with this splendid view was perhaps the roller skating rink towards the north of the ground. To my eyes it seemed an intrusion alongside the unencumbered green. The club had already disallowed entertainments such as Houghton's Poultry Shows on the ground, once immensely popular among the working people the south of the Thames. I wished, perhaps uncharitably, that the roller skating rink would disappear as well, and set up somewhere else where it did not distract from the cricket, to be frequented by folks partial to that sort of amusement.

The pitch, however, still looked extremely wet. It would be a hard task for the bowlers to run in when play did start, and I did suffer from some doubts about how the England bowlers would bear up in these conditions.

Having looked around the ground, my eyes returned to rove about the pavilion. Beside me, Holmes had his eyes affixed to a pair of French-made, Merchant Marine binoculars, observing the crowd with great concentration. Around us, the members of the Surrey Club were filtering into the room, with energetic steps, eager to watch a great day of cricket.

It was then that I suddenly suffered an involuntary shudder. Just outside one of the doors stood a long, lean form, donning the Australian blazer and cricket cap bearing the red, black and yellow colours of the 96th regiment. The drooping moustache and the long hooked nose bestowed on him a distinctly Mephistophelian look, while the eyes that seemed to penetrate into my insides burned with a force beyond anything known to man. This was Spofforth, a man I had seen often enough in the ground, but never at such close quarters. Why, I asked myself, was he looking at me with that degree of unwavering concentration?

But, soon enough, The Demon turned and walked away, disappearing into the corridor that led up to the Australian dressing room. I felt as if his gaze had left holes inside me that seemed to crackle and burn long after he had gone.

On the other side of the room, in front of another door, I was fascinated to notice the England captain AN Hornby himself, absorbed in conversation with someone just out of my sight. During the course of their discussion, the other man moved and I was almost out of my seat in excitement as the giant form of WG came into view, complete with his great black beard. At this moment, as a near-juvenile fascination gripped my joyous heart, Mr Alcock approached us.

"Mr Holmes, Dr Watson, I am most grateful that you came over early in spite of the weather. The match, I daresay, will not resume before midday. In the meantime, Mr Holmes, have you made any progress in the matter?"

Rising from his seat, Holmes replied with the easy courtesy for which he was so remarkable. "There is no need to worry at present, Mr Alcock. Yet, I do have a question or two for you. Could you tell me which of the current group of Australian players and the managers accompanying them have communicated with you in writing? Be it on this occasion or when they had visited earlier in 1880 or 1878 or even in letters sent from Australia between these years."

"But, Mr Holmes, quite a few of them have. Murdoch the captain has certainly communicated, as have Mr Horan, Mr Garrett, Mr Boyle. I remember the Club receiving letters from Percy McDonnell and, the last time, Spoff as well. Besides that, the organisers have corresponded a great deal. That includes Arthur Blake, James Stewart and the travelling manager, Charles Beal, all men belonging to the legal profession. Apart from that, there are Edmund Parkes, Superintendent of the Bank of Australia, and Frederick Dangar and Caleb Peacock, established businessmen from Adelaide and Sydney."

"Thank you, Mr Alcock, you have been thorough as usual."

Mr Alcock bowed slightly and then dropped his voice to a whisper. "As I told you yesterday, gentlemen, the Lancashire press is still up in arms against us. Look at this," he handed us a copy of the day's *Manchester Guardian*, pointing to an article. Taking hold of the newspaper, I found that a correspondent, giving his name as CFN, Old Trafford, had written:

"Sir,

I cannot but regret that Crossland and Pilling have been debarred from upholding against our strong opponents the dignity, honour and ability, of, once more the premier county of England … On the first visit of Spofforth with the Australian Eleven to England, his bowling was of general suspicion and a topic of conversation amongst cricketers simply because he displayed such remarkable performances with the ball, and for no other reason. And so it is with Crossland, whose performances this season stamp him as one of the fastest and at the same time, fairest bowlers of England."

There was another letter echoing the same sentiments from 'Cover Point'. Yet another writer, calling himself 'Middle Stump', cited Crossland's bowling figures against Australia during the tour as 7 for 72 in 49.3 overs and vehemently rejected the notion that his action was suspect. "As for getting his wickets by mere brute force, one would almost think from such an epithet that Crossland walks across to the batsmen, knocks them down and plucks the stumps up, instead of bowling from the opposite end."

"You see gentlemen," Mr Alcock went on. "The very fact that the paper publishes so many letters on the same theme gives away their slant. It is one reason why I may have seemed unusually sensitive to any scandal that may occur at The Oval."

Our client hastened away with an apology as demands on his time as the master of ceremonies at The Oval were numerous. He was called away this time at the request of the distinguished grey-haired Bob Thoms, one of the umpires standing in the game, presumably to discuss the time of start of play and the modified timing of the luncheon interval.

My friend turned towards me. "I assume it is redundant, Watson, but I will ask you to keep your eyes peeled on the action in the middle. I may be leaving your side quite often today to venture into the different stands, enclosures and embankments around the ground, but use your knowledge of this strange game to the fullest and try to determine if there are any strange goings on within the field of play."

Having passed on his instructions, Holmes got up from his chair and made his way out of the room with long strides. I resumed my scrutiny of the ground and the peripheries. The roofs of the buildings in the ground were filling up. The roof of the tavern was full to the brim. The refreshments, which included tumblers of beer, were already in circulation. The excitement bristled around the ground with every passing moment that brought the start closer.

"We do revel in a close match, sir, but I tell you, we won't get one. These Colonials will be beaten easily and well. In my day, sir, we could have beaten them yesterday, but the decadence that has spread in English cricket in the past few decades will make us sweat for another day. However, we will beat them easily, sir, you'll see."

An elderly member had slipped into the seat next to me and had addressed me with these words. The whiteness of his whiskers spoke of a sunny youth spent watching Fuller

Pilch stroke the ball in the middle, batting under his top hat. I had a fair deal to say about the excellence of the Australian team, the way they had beaten MCC in 1878, and of Spofforth's bowling on the previous day, but long experience has taught me that the flowers of one's romantic youth continue to be in full and brightest bloom long after they have withered, and the fields full of the fresh daisies of the current day seem barren in contrast to the brightly painted past. So I forced a smile and told him that I was sure that he was right.

"Ah, that may be a blunder!" another voice sounded from the distant corner of the room and, following it, I could make out that Lord Harris was looking agitated. "The conditions will make it near impossible for the bowlers to run in. Gripping the ball is going to be a challenge."

It transpired that Hornby had agreed to a start within a few minutes. The heavy roller was already being pulled across the wicket by the horse.

Whatever the misgivings of Lord Harris, a great cheer went up around the ground as the six English amateur cricketers emerged from the pavilion and made their way onto the ground. A couple of minutes later, the crowd erupted again as the five professional players ran into the field to make up the eleven.

Next, somewhat to my surprise, the spectators cheered heartily as the two Australian opening batsmen, Alick Bannerman and Hugh Massie, walked to the wicket.

CHAPTER 7

MASSIE HITS OUT

I LOOKED around the field. The towering form of WG stood at point. Lyttleton was behind the wicket. At mid-off I recognised Maurice Read, the man who had been chosen ahead of Crossland, a selection that was so unacceptable to the Lancastrians. Hornby had handed the ball to Barlow, who would bowl with his back to us. At the wicket, Bannerman looked around the field, gave his cap a tug and prepared to take strike.

The venerable gentleman beside me remarked, "Take heed, sir, they will struggle to make England bat again."

"But they need only 38 to do so."

The old man waved a gnarled hand. "I have seen many a game in my time, sir, when teams have been bowled out for less than that."

As if to mock him, Bannerman cut the first ball past point for two. He was in some sort of trouble with the fourth ball of the over, as it went streakily through the slips for two more runs. Yet, every notch they made was vital, and the first over underlined that running in on that slippery, damp ground and maintaining a good line with the wet ball were going to be very difficult.

From the Gasometer End, it was Ulyett who was entrusted with the bowling. One could almost see the mud splashing as the Yorkshire all-rounder made his way to the crease with the ball. Massie made his intentions abundantly clear as he drove the second ball deep into the off-side. The dampness of the ground slowed the speed of the ball considerably and Read hared after it. The batsmen crossed over twice and were turning for the third when the Surrey man hurled his throw in to Lyttleton. Why he chose to throw to the far end, I will never know. The wicketkeeper broke the stumps but Bannerman was home, and dry but for his muddy boots. If Read had thrown to the near end, to Ulyett, Massie would have had no chance of making it in time.

Was this a lapse suspicious enough for me to report to Holmes? I sought to make a detached judgement and thought about the excitement that overcomes one during a keen contest on the sporting field. The error was one which most sportsmen could have committed, I thought, coaxing myself to be vigilant but not all prey to excessive suspicion.

While I thought about it, Massie had cut Barlow high over the head of Barnes at point. In ordinary circumstances, the ball would have reached the boundary at lightning speed, but the ground was wet. Barnes almost overtook the trickling orb of red as it reached the fence. Thoms signalled the boundary and the over was bowled. Massie was on 7 from just 6 balls. The plans were transparent enough to the thinking spectator. As long as the wicket was easier than usual, Massie would hit. The sun would soon be drying it and make batting the most difficult ordeal in the world. If Australia could get a sizeable score by then, England would be set a tricky target when the pitch was at its worst. The Oval wicket was said to be best when drenched, diabolical when drying.

The word 'diabolical' flitting through my mind gave me cause to remember the eyes of The Demon. Had he been looking at me? Why? Or did he have this effect on anyone who caught that burning and hypnotic glare?

Barlow had problems in approaching the wicket across the slushy turf. Frantic signals were made, and the groundsman John Newton emerged with a spade. The bowling holes were adjusted, mud was removed and plenty of sawdust applied. However, it did not seem to help our bowler.

Barlow's next over saw Massie clip him in front of square on the leg side for three. The old gentleman next to me launched into a long diatribe on the plummeting standards of English cricket. The great Surrey bowlers of the past would never have tolerated such audacity in a Colonial. I thought of reminding him that perhaps the greatest of the older Surrey cricketers, William Caffyn, had himself settled in Australia, and coached at Melbourne while making his living as a hairdresser. Maybe he had a hand in the impressive showing of the Colonials? As I watched the proceedings from this vantage viewpoint, a part of my mind wondered to where Holmes had wandered off.

There were a couple of mis-hits and a couple of anxious moments for Massie against Ulyett. But when he hit the Yorkshire professional to square leg for four and in the next over launched Barlow over square leg for another boundary, the Australians were on 25 in almost no time. A bit more of this and they would be taking the match away.

Hornby was obviously as worried about the situation as any other man. He changed the bowling from both ends. Peate came on from Ulyett's end, and Studd from Barlow's. Bannerman had, for all intents and purposes, decided to offer the dead bat, but Massie carried on with his explosive batting, on-driving Studd for a boundary. He followed it with another forceful drive but Studd quickly moved across to stop it with some splendid athleticism much to the delight of the spectators. There was still no sign of Holmes.

As runs were scored, the faces in the pavilion became glum. Lord Harris sat with the other selectors with a pensive expression on his face. I could see Charles Alcock at the rear of the room, the tension of the match perhaps eclipsing his concern about the warning message he had received. He looked a man burdened with several cares, though his eyes were riveted to the field of play.

I looked around for the binoculars Holmes had brought with him, but he seemed to have taken them. Even if he were among the crowd, it would be impossible to pick him out with the naked eye. Meanwhile, Massie crossed over with a hasty run and focused his tactics on the left-arm spin of Peate. He hit the Yorkshire slow bowler hard and high, almost straight, to the on-side boundary. In Peate's next over, after Bannerman had batted out his usual maiden, Massie off-drove him into the crowd, deep inside the row of spectators standing on the embankment. Play had commenced just about 30 minutes earlier and Massie was already on 33. Australia were 38 without losing a man, level with the England total. The advantage had been efficiently erased, and if one took into account the effect that the sun was going to have on the wicket, Australia were definitely at an advantage now.

As if to celebrate, Massie drove Studd straight to the boundary. Even the refined atmosphere of the pavilion was disturbed by a couple of plebeian groans. One of the members, face flushed with consternation, was demonstrating the science of playing the drive and the way a bowler could work his way around the bat, and he did so by gripping his walking stick with considerable vigour and using it as a proxy of the willow.

Now the erstwhile inert and inactive Bannerman cut Peate twice, one of them rather fortuitously, getting two runs each time for his efforts. It was 47 without anything to show for the efforts of the fielding side. Hornby's troubles could be sensed even from the pavilion where we sat. Studd was removed from the attack and Barnes put on.

With his incredible grasp of the game, Lord Harris half rose from his seat, as if certain that something out of the ordinary was about to take place. It was indeed so. Massie had been inclined to stamp his authority on every new bowler from the very first ball. He tried to repeat this with Barnes, hitting him long and hard towards the off side.

All eyes followed the trajectory of the ball as the local favourite, 'Bunny' Lucas, got under it at long-off. The next moment young Lucas had metamorphosed from hero to villain. The ball had slipped through his fingers and dropped at his feet. Groans and hoots of disappointment rippled across the ground, and I would be failing in the historical accuracy of my account if I did not add that a couple of blasphemous expressions rang out the hallowed atmosphere of the pavilion. The man whose bat was proving to be a dangerous weapon against all of England had just been granted another life. Bannerman now cut Barnes for two to bring up the 50 in just 35 minutes. The applause was full of good spirit and warmth, but there was no doubt that the England supporters were getting worried.

What did I make of the error by Lucas? As if on cue Sherlock Holmes made his way across the room and lowered himself into the chair next to me. "I assume you are not too patriotic, Watson, to the extent that you fail to enjoy the match because of the progress made by the Australians?"

"Holmes, I must admit I am not entirely happy with the situation, but the innings of Massie is indeed a pleasure to witness. But did you notice the spilled catch by Lucas? It was easy enough to have been caught by a fielder far less able than he."

Holmes waved his hand dismissively. "I'm sure you've played enough cricket to be aware that chances do end up on the grass. It is one of those inexplicable parts of the game and lends itself to so many idiomatic expressions. Never allow your foreknowledge to guide the course of imagination, Watson. We balance probabilities and choose the most likely. It is the scientific use of the imagination. And in this case, there is not sufficient evidence to conclude that it was anything other than the commonplace bungling of a catch. Now, if such lapses occur with great frequency, I would be inclined to watch the blunders more closely."

Meanwhile Massie had celebrated his fortuitous escape with a boundary drilled over the head of Barlow off the bowling of Peate. After an uncertain mishit, he drove again, but this time the frantic speed of Allan Steel kept it from reaching the boundary again.

Perhaps Hornby sensed something in Steele's movements, for he was put on in place of Peate.

I turned to Holmes. "Did you find anything out of the ordinary in the ground during your excursion just now?"

"There is no sign of money staked to the extent that it would fit into the category of the extraordinary, Watson, but with my experience in these matters the definition of ordinary may be stretched beyond common usage. Till now I have noticed nothing sinister, yet I am not absolutely certain that the ground is altogether clear of multiple agents of mischief. It seems to me increasingly likely that a mastermind may be at play here, with enough grasp over the subject of mathematical probability to make a considerable fortune out of the ebbs and flows that we see at every moment in this incredibly uncertain match. Yet, he is one who has mastered enough of the science of integral calculus and infinite summations to channel his operations in little, near negligible but startlingly many pockets, so that they do not raise suspicions but can combine into an enormous financial venture."

"Holmes," I said in a hoarse whisper as Massie hit Steel for two to square leg. "Then you know the identity of the man we are dealing with?"

"No, Watson. I am not near to identifying who this genius is. But I do see his hand, a pattern, in many of the crimes that are committed around London. There have been forgeries, murders, robberies, which all carry his signature, but the man himself is never in the vicinity of the actual operations. I can assure you that he will be nowhere near The Oval even today as we study and discuss his handiwork in the field of bookmaking. Some day, I will break through his veil, but I am afraid that day seems rather distant. For now, we have to deal with the minions who carry out his orders, who are dancing to the pull of his invisible strings like veritable puppets."

Holmes broke off as a loud cheer greeted another legside stroke by Massie, and the batsmen ran two. It took the enterprising Australian batsman to his fifty, scored in just 47 minutes, as the clock pointed to just a little before one o'clock. It had been an innings of great adventure, the more pronounced when looked at in conjunction with Bannerman's score of just 11. There had been eight boundary hits in the innings and every stroke a statement of intention.

The celebration of this landmark scarcely had an effect on Bannerman, who calmly played out another maiden over off Barnes.

Steel, his slow-medium deliveries proving to be increasingly accurate, was starting to make an impression. Massie, despite his obvious intention to destroy each new bowler, had not really been able to get on top of this young man from Lancashire. I could almost foresee that he was going to venture on all-out attack, and mentioned it to Holmes.

"I believe you, Watson. If there ever was a consulting detective in matters related to what takes place on the field in cricket, you would find your true calling." I could not make out for sure whether this statement was made in jest or earnest.

Nevertheless, Massie heaved the second ball of Steel's new over to the square leg boundary and Barlow's furious pursuit could not keep it from reaching the fence. He rushed out to the next delivery as well, aiming for exactly the same region. But Steel had cannily mixed up the speed of the balls, and Massie missed it. The faster ball struck the leg-stump, uprooting it out of the ground. It had taken almost an hour, but England had finally made their mark on the scoreboard. Massie walked back for a valiant 55, scored in just 57 minutes from 60 deliveries, and the ground rose in applause as he left. It occurred to me that the wicket had not really been as docile after some twenty minutes of play. Yet, Massie had batted like a seasoned champion.

Murdoch, the Australian captain, obviously thought more could be made by capitalising on the current conditions. As we sat, the huge, god-like form of George Bonnor was seen making his way to the wicket. The thinking in their camp was perhaps that there was still merit in Massie's tactics. The great hitter was therefore promoted in the order and sent forth, obviously with instructions to destroy the bowling. On this present tour, this incredibly handsome man had already hit WG out of the ground at Twickenham and Alfred Shaw out of Trent Bridge. When the Australians had defeated the Gentlemen of England at this very ground, he had scored a fine 74, with three of his fours hit well over the boundary.

It was a most critical juncture, since with a few muscular hits Bonnor could wreak a degree of havoc from which England could find it impossible to recover. Hornby, perhaps fearful of the effect that the giant could have on the slow bowling of Steel, placed his faith in the most experienced professional in his ranks. Ulyett was handed the ball before long. His fourth ball pitched on length, was fast and broke a little. Bonnor's middle stump was knocked out of the ground, resulting in a great roar from the crowd.

"There is a man with a slightly tarnished reputation, but the heart of a lion," Holmes remarked as Ulyett celebrated. "Watson, I sense there will be much activity in many pockets in the ground and around London. Two quick wickets will lead to all sorts of variations in the bookmaking world."

Murdoch now walked to the wicket, cheered all the way by the excellent crowd. But even before the Australian captain had faced a ball, Bannerman, who had batted in a manner to suggest growing roots into the wicket, now hit Barnes high into the air. The secure form of CP Studd got under the ball and made the catch. It was 70 for 3. The smiles that had vanished from the faces in the pavilion now returned, enhanced and widened. The old gentleman next to me, who had been reading the final rites of English cricket for the past hour, looked at me with eyes that seemed to ask the question, "What did I tell you?"

"You don't look very pleased, Watson," Holmes asked with a sense of puzzlement.

"I am happy, Holmes; but if we think ahead, the wicket is obviously back to its devilish ways. If it is this difficult to bat, another fifty or so runs will make it very testing for our men. I say this with full knowledge of the presence of Mr Grace in our ranks."

As if to attest to my views, Tom Horan pushed at Peate and gave a low but gentle catch to Grace at point. Off the very next ball, the supremely talented young George Giffen repeated Horan's stroke and walked back, caught in a similar manner by Grace.

"I must say, Watson, I find your intuition oddly disturbing. It does tell me that with passionate interest and belief in your own deductive powers you can guide your gift in cricket to the detection of crime as well. Here comes what, if I am not mistaken, is called the hat-trick delivery."

Indeed, Jack Blackham had come in to avert a possible hat-trick, a feat Spofforth had accomplished when our men had been down in Australia in 1878-79. The ground watched in rapt attention, except for our garrulous old neighbour who had launched into a detailed description of how round-arm fast bowler James Street had achieved his hat-trick split across two overs in 1868. Alas, the ball

Peate sent down was a rank long hop which the Australian wicketkeeper calmly dispatched to the long leg boundary.

Experience now reigned in the middle as the seasoned play of Murdoch and Blackham kept danger at bay and carried the score along to 99 for 5 at a quarter to two. Holmes had once again set off on one of his excursions around the ground, and my grizzled new friend was trying to regale me with stories about HH Stephenson when the skies opened up again. The players scurried back to the pavilion, and it was announced that lunch would be taken.

CHAPTER 8

TALES OF THE VOYAGE

CHARLES ALCOCK came up to me as I got up from my chair with the intention of stretching my legs and also putting some safe, if temporary, distance between myself and my companion. In the last few minutes, the venerable gentleman was giving all the indications of being as sticky as the wicket in the middle.

"I only wish the rest of the day to be as free of trouble as it has been thus far, Dr Watson," the Surrey secretary said in a voice full of hope. "Where is Mr Holmes?"

I informed him that my friend had gone on another of his walks to keep an eye on things.

"I will be forever indebted to him for the industry he has shown in helping me today. I was just about to ask you to come over for lunch."

"I think I will wait a while for my friend to return. But, Mr Alcock, if I may ask, do you think we are in a good enough position? True, they are just 61 ahead with five wickets down, but in such a tight game does it seem we have things under control?"

Mr Alcock looked even more worried than he had been yesterday. "You never know, Dr Watson. Strange things can happen in cricket, which makes it the king of games that it is."

There was no sign of my friend as I paced about the room, looking at the paintings of old cricket matches. Slowly, however, I gave in to the protests of my stomach and the smells that wafted in from the Member's Dining Room and I went in search of food. As I sat down to a spread of roast beef, Yorkshire pudding and new potatoes, it was with great surprise that I saw Holmes sitting at a table, deep in conversation with a dignified, well-dressed gentleman.

"Watson," he exclaimed as his keen eyes observed me regarding him with what must have been less than the friendliest of expressions. "Allow me to introduce you to Mr Caleb Peacock, former mayor of Adelaide."

The remarkable mask of charm that my friend could put on over his normal somewhat withdrawn persona could be most beguiling at times. With the hearty permission of Mr Peacock I joined them at their table and began eating with considerable gusto. The gentleman was an Australian, one of the financiers of the tour, one of the speculators who provided the money that allowed teams to travel overseas and enabled international cricket to be played between England and the Colonials.

"Mr Peacock was just telling me about the most interesting voyage the Australian party made on the *Assam*," Holmes informed me in a voice full of bonhomie. "The tales of the Christy Minstrel performance and the fancy dress ball have been most entertaining to say the least."

Caleb Peacock laughed with great mirth.

"And don't forget, sir, the performances of *ASS* and *Done on Both Sides* where I had the hilarious duty of being both the stage manager and the prompter; that is the most important role. Although Horan wrote in *The Australasian* that my role as the prompter was seldom needed, nothing can be further from the truth. To add to that, during the Christy Minstrel performance, I had to fill in as the centre-man and the accompanist."

Holmes laughed as I have seldom heard him laugh before, except on occasions when he had performed one of his successful chemical experiments.

"The Australian cricketers and their companions do indeed seem to have talents that go beyond batting and bowling."

"Indeed, sir, the captain Billy Murdoch has a career on the stage for the taking if his phenomenal gifts with the bat ever decline. In the Minstrel show, he teamed up with Charlie Beal, faces blackened with burnt cork and porter. They combined to form a fantastical Bones and Tambo. During the fancy dress too, Murdoch was the most convincing as a monk. Most of the men dressed up as cricketers, I must say that there is little surprise in that, but Bannerman played a naval officer. Bonnor, with a hideous blanket on his shoulders, was rather patchy as an ancient Roman soldier. But Murdoch as the monk was impeccable. He even upstaged Spoff, who, as you can very well guess, played the Mephistopheles, almost to life."

While the memory of the gaze of The Demon yet made my stomach turn, Holmes once again laughed long and hard.

"It is rumoured that The Demon has developed a conscientious habit of rigorous training on this voyage. Is it true that he went all the way to Mitcham Green to perfect his break-backs even yesterday, before the start of the match?"

Mr Peacock gave the impression of being surprised. "Oh dear, has that also made its way to the press? Why, indeed sir, Spoff was most adamant in his desire to practice yesterday. Beal and Blake did reason with him, but he had set his heart and soul on it. In the end he did go down to Southerton's place to bowl his demonic balls. Perhaps that will lead us to a famous victory today."

"We will have to wait for that, sir, the rain is just about holding up. I must say it is rather perilous to allow so important a player to wander around in London on the day of the match. It is a confusing city. We have had players from other counties who, coming here to play Surrey, got lost on the way, turning up several hours late."

Mr Peacock laughed. "Oh, Spoff knows London well enough. This is not the first time he has been here. Besides, we did not let him wander alone. Beal and Blake went with him, as did McDonnell, although he kept complaining that he was too sick. Spoff wanted someone to bat as he went through his experiments."

I glanced at Holmes, who gave no indication of triumph as the names of the Australian party at Southerton were revealed to us. The conversation now somehow turned to rowing, a sport in which Mr Peacock was extremely interested. Holmes tactfully got up, leaving me to appear engrossed in the topic of boats and oars which held scarcely any fascination for me.

CHAPTER 9

DEATH BEFORE WICKET

THE RAIN, heaven be blessed, was not heavy and by half past two the sun was out and shining. I resumed my seat in front of the pavilion window and Holmes was out on another of his errands when play began again. Peate bowled from the Gasometer End and his first two balls were too good for Blackham to touch. The interruption had somehow made batting an even more arduous endeavour, and with the fourth ball Peate found the edge and Lyttleton pulled off a smart catch low down to his right. The crowd, still moving around in the aftermath of the break, was delighted with this immediate success, and the cheers were loud and raucous.

There now began a period of cautious battle for survival. Murdoch, using all his experience, was holding down one end, taking the odd run when it was opportune. Young Sammy Jones, playing only because McDonnell was not, was fully occupied trying to keep his wicket intact. There was one cross-batted stroke through the covers for four, but other than that Jones did not give any indication of being comfortable at the crease.

"The batsmen of today are not geared for situations like this," muttered the old gentleman to my right. "He will be gone any minute now."

The score limped along to 114, proving that Massie's innings had been but a welcome exception to the rule of slow, dogged batting throughout the match. This was how it was when the curious incident occurred that has gone down as one of the most infamous in history.

Murdoch was facing Steel bowling from the Pavilion End, and played an unconvincing uppish push to the leg side. There was no short leg in place, and the ball landed out of harm's way; by the time the agile Lyttleton had scurried across to retrieve it, the run was completed. Grace, coming in from short point, was at the wicket, and Lyttleton threw to him. The young Jones, feeling safe in the belief that the ball was dead, was patting down a divot on the wicket. At this moment the Champion, his quick eyes noticing that the lad was outside his crease, broke the wicket and appealed.

The men in the middle were as surprised as the officials, and not all the members sitting in the pavilion approved. Umpire Thoms gestured and spoke, and eventually raised his finger. The ball, which Jones had taken for dead, had been alive. On grounds of legality the appeal could not be questioned, but the series of gasps in the pavilion, the mixture of scattered applause and a round of boos across the ground, and the enraged noises that could be heard from the Australian dressing room told me eloquently enough that there were plenty of doubts about the spirit in which the act had been performed.

To my lasting surprise, my companion in the chair was pink with laughter. "Why sir, the Champion taught the young lad a valuable lesson," he managed to say between chuckles.

Jones did not look up even for a moment as he trudged back to the pavilion in abject disappointment. There came the sound of heavy angry footsteps and I saw The Demon walking out to bat. I only saw his back, but there was no doubt that under the gold, black and red cap, his eyes burned as he bristled with indignation.

I stole a couple of glances at the faces of Lord Harris and Charles Alcock. They did not betray any emotion, but I wondered if they were happy with what had taken place. The wicket was important, but the price at which it came, bordering on straining the relationship between the sides, was perhaps too steep to pay.

Before the turmoil had a chance to play itself out, Spofforth was dismissed, Peate's delivery beating him and striking the middle stump. Australia led by 79 and there were just two wickets left.

Garrett was the new man who walked to the wicket, but the over had ended and Steel bowled to Murdoch. I saw just enough to witness the Australian captain driving to the on and Ulyett moving fast to keep the score down to a solitary run. At this moment there was a tap on my shoulder. Charles Alcock's worried face was looking at me in ardent appeal.

"Dr Watson, would you be kind enough to come up to the room upstairs? Something terrible has happened."

The tone of his voice left me in no doubt about the urgency of the situation. I quickly got to my feet, leaving unheard the story of the cricketer Julius Caesar that my old companion had started recounting. Following Mr Alcock with quick steps up the stairs, we reached a small room where a couple of pavilion attendants stood with grave faces. On a makeshift bed assembled by joining a couple of sofas lay a man of some forty or so years, dressed in the attire of a respectable clerk, slightly dishevelled and dreadfully still.

"Could you as a medical man please take a look at him, Dr Watson?" Mr Alcock asked. I had already advanced towards the man, feeling for his pulse. There was none that I could find, either in the veins of the wrist or at the throat. He was dead and beyond the reach of any assistance, medical or otherwise.

"I am afraid the man is past any help. How did this happen?"

Mr Alcock looked distinctly weary in the face of all the diverse troubles that were continuing to plague his day. "He was sitting in the terraced annexe and had told a couple of other spectators that he was suffering from a pain in his chest, was not really feeling well. He was about to get up to leave the ground when he fell, clutching his chest. A couple of stewards were alerted and they brought him here."

"Is there someone here among those who sat around him?" The question was voiced from the door. I looked around to find Holmes standing at the threshold, looking with intense concentration at the dead man.

One of the stewards answered, "No sir, they are out in the stands. We carried the gentleman here."

Holmes looked at him. "And what's that you have in your hand, my lad?"

"The hat and the coat of the gentleman, sir. We tried to revive him while he lay in the stands."

There was the sound of rushing footsteps and all of a sudden EM Grace pushed his way through the entrance. "What is it, Charles? What goes on?"

"This poor man died watching the game, EM. I'd be glad if you would take a look. I already have Dr Watson here, offering his professional opinion."

The cricketer glanced at the dead man who lay in front of us.

"What an ugly business," EM Grace remarked with feeling. "Poor soul. He only wanted to enjoy a good day's cricket."

"Yes, God bless his soul," said Mr Alcock.

"Perhaps," sounded the voice of Holmes.

"Perhaps what?" EM turned around sharply. "And you, sir, are …?"

"This is my friend, Mr Sherlock Holmes," Mr Alcock hastened to explain. "You certainly know Dr EM Grace. We are lucky to have him with us today, because apart from being a great cricketer and a medical doctor, EM is a coroner for the lower division of Gloucestershire. The peculiar circumstances of this death will obviously result in an inquest. The coroner of East Surrey will be involved. It might be useful to have an immediate first-hand opinion from men like Dr Watson and Dr Grace."

EM Grace looked at the stewards. "Could you get a couple of the spectators who sat next to him to come here?"

"Yes sir." As the men started to leave, Holmes added, "And check whether there are any belongings of the gentleman which may still be lying there?"

The elder Grace brother approached the body and inspected it closely. "Classic symptoms of a weak heart, my dear sir?"

It took me a while to realise that the great EM Grace was actually consulting me over a subject of common specialisation. It was as if from a trance that my voice answered, "Yes, it looks that way to me. We can confirm when the eyewitnesses arrive, but it does seem ..."

I broke off as a great tumult of cheering drowned my words.

"What in God's name has happened out there? Can someone please let me know?" EM Grace shouted.

Mr Alcock was equally affected, all his instincts urging him to run out and check what was happening on the field of play.

"He's out, sir," a voice of a steward announced.

"Who's out, my good man? Could you please tell me the whole story?" EM thundered back.

A new steward peeped inside the room. "Mr Murdoch, sir. Mr Garrett hit one through cover, and Mr Hornby chased it down. He was run out as they went for the third run."

"I'll hardly believe that, my good man," EM Grace sounded irritated. "Monkey can't throw a cricket ball to please a dying grandmother, any more than I can throw an elephant. You mean to say he threw it all the way back to Lyttleton?"

There was a muffled chuckle. "Nay sir, Mr Murdoch seemed to think as you did that Mr Hornby could not throw the ball. But Mr Hornby cleverly jerked the ball to Mr Studd, and he sent in a long return to the keeper, sir."

"By Jove, that's jolly good play." The coroner seemed pleased.

"It certainly is. How much did Murdoch make?" asked Alcock.

"Honestly, sir, I can't quite decide what to make of the lot of you," Holmes sounded a trifle peeved at this exchange. "A man lies dead out here and you are discussing the score of Murdoch?"

EM Grace looked at him sharply. "Why, Mr Holmes, here is a case of death. Out there it is a matter of life and death. There is life in the match yet, but this man cannot be helped, he is already gone. Dr Watson agrees that he died from a weak heart."

I looked at the man again. "There are some abrasions near the temple."

The coroner followed my eyes. "Yes, I see them. No doubt caused when he fell."

"I'd agree," I said. "He seems to have complained of chest pain, and fell down clutching his chest. Here come our men."

Even as the stewards returned, ushering in a couple of men, a great cry rang through.

"There's the last of them," said one of the newcomers. "Boyle must have gone first ball."

EM looked sternly at them. "By how much do they lead?"

"Why, sir, a mere 84. With the great WG in the side, it will be child's play."

"How much did Murdoch make?"

"29, sir, and superb runs they were too."

"I'm sure they were. On this wicket, that's as good as Massie's innings or even better."

"They better knock these runs off, sir. I have a fair amount on England."

EM scoffed.

"Say, sir, aren't you the Little Doctor? WG's brother? I've watched you open England's innings with WG when the Australians were here in '80."

It was Charles Alcock who put matters in perspective with an astute intervention.

"Gentlemen, this is indeed Dr EM Grace. But could you tell us what happened to this poor man here?"

The two looked at the dead man and tried hard to transform their excitement into a semblance of seriousness.

"Why, sir, he was there since the morning, recording the score with much diligence. Nothing seemed wrong with him. It was only after the luncheon that he behaved in this fidgety way. Clutched his chest, said he was having a problem breathing. And then he got up, saying he had to go, and dropped just like that, still clutching his chest."

Holmes was busy, trotting noiselessly about the room, sometimes stopping, sometimes kneeling, once lying flat on his face. EM looked at him in the oddest of ways. "What on earth is this gentleman up to?"

My friend did not respond to the question, but proceeded with one of his own. "Who took off his hat?"

"Pardon me, sir?" the men from the stands were slightly confused.

"Come, come, sir, a simple question if there ever was one. Play began after lunch with the sun shining brightly, the terraced stands are without a cover at the top and at three o'clock or thereabouts the sun is high. There is no shade in that part of the ground. This gentleman must have had his hat on, given that he was carrying a wide-brimmed one for this very purpose. Who took it off?"

One of the stewards replied, "As I said already, sir, we had taken the hat off, as also the coat, in an effort to revive him."

"So when you arrived he was lying on the ground?"

"Lying in the stands, sir."

"And his hat was on his head?"

"Yes, sir."

"It had not been knocked off by the fall?"

"No, sir."

"Did this gentleman sit all through the morning in the same place?"

"Hard to tell, sir," replied one of the spectators. "He must've taken a break or two to relieve himself at least. Can't say for sure."

"Thank you, gentlemen," Holmes turned to the steward. "If you don't mind, lad, once you have escorted the gentlemen back to their seats, can you come back to the pavilion room? You could be of valuable use." Holmes fished out a shilling and tossed it across.

"Thank you very much, sir, I will."

Once the men had left, Holmes turned to EM Grace. "The death, as both of you have mentioned, could well have been due to a sudden affliction of the heart. Yet, the marks at the temple could not have been caused by the fall. With a hat of that wide a brim on his head, it is impossible that he hit his temple that hard so as to cut it open, and still kept the hat on the head."

As was often the case with Holmes, the irrefutability of the logic rendered any argument on our part futile. Even EM Grace knew that Holmes had an incontestable point.

"I am prone to agree, but in any case the marks on the head are not violent enough to result in fatality. And it does not tally with this man's complaints or his manner of falling to his death."

"Exactly. There are other singular points in this matter. In the pocket of the coat that our steward so thoughtfully removed, I found this pocketbook. Among other things, it contains a printed score card, where one can jot down whatever goes on during the day. A most baffling pastime if you ask me, but with significant usefulness in a situation like the present. One might expect to see a thorough documentation. Here, our deceased friend has diligently put down every detail until the score reached 62 without a wicket. After that, one encounters a break in his record. By the time the regular jottings are resumed, the score is 79 for five. Watson, was it not ticking towards one in the afternoon when Massie reached his half-century?"

EM Grace looked rather confused, and I could not blame him. Even long association with Holmes has not made me immune to surprise at his sudden exposition of a sequence of logical moves piecing together the solution to a problem.

Charles Alcock's face mingled uneasiness and doubt in great proportions.

"Mr Holmes, do you think this is not death by natural causes?"

"It is difficult to theorise without the full data, Mr Alcock. However, it does seem that some mischief may have been afoot. Dr Grace, if you were to meet someone at a designated hour, what would be your preferred time? Would you agree to a meeting at 11 o'clock, or is it more likely that it would be, say, ten minutes past the hour?"

EM Grace frowned in confusion. "I don't see much sense in the question, sir. Of course, it would be extremely unlikely for me to fix something at ten past eleven unless there was some definite cause, for example the departure of a train."

"Excellent, Dr Grace, you could not have made a better point. So, my theory is that his break in jotting down the ball-by-ball details halted at one o'clock because he was due to meet someone at that precise hour."

"That's a most incredible suggestion, Mr Holmes." EM did not sound impressed. He would have spoken further had not heavy footsteps been heard, and soon a strapping giant form loomed in our midst. For a while I could not determine whether I was really experiencing the moment or was having an incredible dream.

"What on earth are you doing here? You have a match to win." EM Grace sounded most critical of his younger and rather more gifted brother.

The bearded demi-god of cricket spoke in his high-pitched voice. "I was told to come here, to examine a sick man. Don't worry. There's a delay in any case."

"Don't tell me it's raining again," said the elder Grace irritably.

"No. But Murdoch is not happy with the dismissal of young Jones. He cribs. Now he wants to use the roller, as a way of showing his dissent, and make us fidget a bit."

EM scoffed again. "He is unhappy, is he? Tell him that given the same circumstances, most of his precious men would have done the same."

"Spoff said it will lose us the match."

"He did, now, did he? I can tell him something as well. But, there's nothing for you to do here. The poor man is dead."

For some idiotic reason, at this moment I had thrust my hand out, just to grasp the most famous hand in the land. WG took it in his huge grip with some surprise. "Good afternoon, Dr Grace. I'm Dr Watson, and I have examined the dead man. It seems from the eyewitnesses that he complained of chest pain, clutched his heart and fell… already dead."

"He does display signs of being the typical heart patient. The tension probably did him in." WG peered closely at the deceased man.

"There are some unexplained bruises around the side of the head. Light ones, but they could not have resulted from the fall when his heart gave up."

WG glanced at the temple and ran his fingers lightly over the marks. "Looks like strong abrasions, but not serious enough to stop the heart. No puncture of a vein. No connection with the cause of death as far as I can say. Blimey, probably it happened out of tearing his hair at our miserable attempts to keep Massie from scoring. Poor soul. Cricket is not for the weak of heart. Wish I could have a penny for each time I have said that."

Holmes glanced at the three of us who stood looking at the unfortunate man.

"If a man has a heart condition, is it possible for him to aggravate it suddenly by getting involved in a fight? So that after a while he feels sick and finally he dies from it?"

I agreed that it was possible, and after a while WG nodded as well. "Perhaps, lots of things are possible. I have seen men struck by a cricket ball and pass away days later. Remember George Summers at Lord's in '70? I was on the field but just a medical student at that time. I did what I could, but he fell dead when he reached Nottingham. I believe to this day the train journey had made it worse. But, I have to go now. I did tell them that I was professionally engaged, and the pitch was getting rolled. The horse was playing up when being put into harness, but some of the spectators volunteered to pull the roller themselves. I assume it's done now."

"Watch out for Spoff. He sounds seriously incensed at what you did to Jones."

WG lumbered off and EM turned to Holmes.

"I do follow your train of thought, sir, but I can tell you it is very difficult to get a conviction of manslaughter based on such a tenuous thread."

The remark brought forth a smile on the detective's face. "I assure you, Dr Grace, that is farthest from my thoughts. Thank you for all your help. Mr Alcock, is there somewhere that Dr Watson and I can sit alone and uninterrupted?"

"Of course."

We followed Charles Alcock down the flight of stairs. On our way, we almost ran into the Australian side going out onto the field.

"This thing can be done," a firm voice announced. Looking up, I found myself staring into the very eyes of Spofforth. His gaze remained fixed on me for a brief while before he donned his cap and made his way into the sun.

CHAPTER 10

THE CHASE

THE CLOCK showed a quarter to four and there was a tense hush among the spectators as the Colonials came out onto the field.

Mr Alcock led us to a locked room and opened the door. "This is the committee room. You will remain undisturbed here. But, pray tell me, Mr Holmes, is this death in any way connected to the warning I received yesterday?"

"I have every reason to believe so, but I don't have all the facts yet. Could you please let the steward I spoke to know that I am in this room?"

"Of course, Mr Holmes. I have also called for an ambulance from the London Metropolitan Asylum Board."

"That is the wisest course."

Yonder I could see Dr Grace walk out with our captain, Hornby, slightly surprising since I expected Barlow to open as he had done in the first innings. Holmes, following my gaze, burst out laughing.

"Watson," he said between chuckles. "Till this day I had not been fully abreast of the effect a mere game can have on grown men. But this has been a most educating experience. The coroner is apt to forget the corpse and ask for the score. The responsible secretary, standing between infamy and scandal, wants to know how someone was dismissed. And you, dear Watson, who profess every interest in my cases and have even diligently documented some, you wonder about the English opening combination even when there is every possibility that a murder has taken place."

I tried to look apologetic, but could not stop myself from contradicting him. "But Holmes, the chances of a murder seem minimal. There are some abrasions on the dead man's temple, but it seems a little thing and unrelated to the cause of death."

"Little things are infinitely the most important, Watson. Perhaps the death was not a direct cause of the marks, but we must test theories before discarding them. Let us look at the facts. Bear with me for just a while before you focus your attention on the game again."

Looking out of the window, I saw Blackham standing way back as The Demon marked out his run up, bowling to Grace. Yet, this was the prince of wicketkeepers who stood up to the fastest of them, and had effected a stumping off Spofforth in the first innings. The first ball was enough for me to conclude that Spoff would be bowling at a furious rate. However, for the moment I turned back to Holmes.

"The pocketbook of the deceased man provides us with a veritable cornucopia of facts. Here, Watson, help me piece them together, although I know that yonder Spofforth has a mean and hungry look."

My friend tipped out the contents. Apart from a few shillings, the pocketbook contained a bunch of receipts and vouchers.

"Our late friend was very methodical in keeping the details of his expenses. Here I have one train ticket from London to Plymouth. Another back to London. This is a bill for breakfast at an inn in Oxford, but the man had only toast and coffee."

It hardly made much sense to me. "The man obviously got around, travelled a lot, and did not eat much in the morning. But does it tell us much more?"

"Now this should be interesting. There are several bills from the restaurant at the Tavistock Hotel. Yet, our man goes to this expensive establishment only to have… coffee, coffee, orange juice…"

"The Tavistock Hotel is the place where the Australian team is staying," I cried.

"It is, indeed. And their ship, the *Assam,* docked in Plymouth. Their first trip was made to play Oxford University. I am sure we will find some receipt from the Southerton Hotel as well. Voila, here they are: as many as three visits."

"But the Australians have been up north to Yorkshire, and west to Gloucestershire. They have played in Nottingham as well. Do we have any tickets or bills from there?" By now the problem was revealing itself to be of unusual interest and the cheers that Grace and Barlow drew with the first few runs did not manage to divert my attention.

"As I mentioned in the morning, Watson, we are dealing with a mastermind out there, and our net cast at The Oval can at best fish out a minnow from his huge, complex network. I believe this man, who can in no way be identified from his belongings, was the main operative in London. Since the Australians were to travel to London on arrival, he was entrusted to make contact with them at Plymouth. He probably covered Oxford as well. Every time the Australian team has visited these parts, our late friend has called in at the Tavistock. Yet, he was not a rich man. He seldom had anything more than coffee or a juice. If you look further there are omnibus tickets issued by the London Road Car Company, against fares from Mitcham to Kennington. Perhaps he got reimbursed for his expenses on production of these bills from the man behind the operations. If you looked at his boots, there was ample soil residue to tell me that he had walked a large part of his way from the Tavistock to the Surrey side of the Thames today. Isn't it surprising that someone who cannot afford to hire a hansom and prefers to walk rather than board omnibuses unless the distance is long and time is short, that such a person makes trips to the Tavistock for breakfast?"

"Perhaps he was only a man who hero worshipped the Australian cricketers. There are quite a few of that kind."

"The character type does not quite fit. Neither does the way he filled out the scorebook. Keen, methodical, almost as if maintaining the books of his business. Not a hero worshipper. And no admirer of the Australian team would have left the stands to keep an appointment when Massie was playing that exceptionally fine innings. My theory is that he tried to contact the Australian cricketers, and negotiate with them to set up matches. Perhaps his arrival at Southerton's Hotel ahead of such a key encounter as this great match was the last straw for the particular Australian who sent Mr Alcock the letter."

"Who was that Australian?"

"I am not certain yet, but I do have my suspicions."

A knock on the door interrupted our conversation at this very interesting juncture. Holmes opened the door to find the polite steward eager to offer his services.

"Hold the fort, Watson, keep your eyes peeled, watch the match, and we will soon solve this curious jigsaw."

Left alone, I turned to see Hornby cut a ball from Spofforth late and delectably through the slips to the boundary. England were into double figures. Things looked like going according to plan. A gasp from the huge gathering told me that Grace had come close to being caught and bowled by Garrett. With such slices of luck and some solid batsmanship, 85 runs were but a trifle. The Australians went about stopping the strokes of the two batsmen with the agility and speed of a group of wildcats, but it did seem that they had left themselves too few runs to make a match of it.

My thoughts, though, were more than a little premature. The hour called for a talent head and shoulders above the norm, and in Fred 'The Demon' Spofforth, the Colonials had in their midst just such a man.

After Grace had stroked the ball to the off-side and taken a run off the first ball of this Mephisthophelean bowler's fifth over, this remarkable cricketer ran in with his long, lithe strides, appearing to throw the whole swing of his long arm and his long body into his effort, his limbs a whirlwind of action as he delivered the ball. His body and his arm followed right over until his hand almost touched the ground. The ball broke back from the pitch and struck the top of Hornby's off-stump. It was 15 for one.

The Australians celebrated, and I could see The Demon piercing the new batsman Barlow with his severe eyes. As he marked his guard, the Lancashire all-rounder, perhaps the safest of all England batsmen, had his back to the bowler. Yet, I could see Spofforth still fixing him with his sinister stare. There was something eerily supernatural about the powers of this man.

If anyone could hold one end up for England, as Bannerman had done so admirably for Australia while Massie had stroked with jaunty abandon, it was Barlow. Grace was there with his mammoth presence at one end, but a lot of our hopes rested with the stone-waller. Spofforth ran in again, pitching the ball outside the off, cutting it in with vicious skill. Barlow got a thin bit of his bat on the ball, and it crashed off the edge onto his off and middle stumps. The Colonials could hardly hide their delight. Even as Barlow walked back to the pavilion, his journey out and back having yielded nothing to show for his efforts, the eyes of Spofforth seemed to be trained on him. I remembered the way he had looked at me during the day. But, whatever it was that aroused the frightening, uneasy sensation and made my hair stand on end, Spofforth was not doing anything suspicious as far as the cricket was concerned. His performance had not been tampered with by any earthly force. If at all, it had been done by the hand of God, or the Devil himself.

For some obscure reason, I now marvelled at the nerves of the dead man. If Holmes had been right about him, and I have seldom known my friend to be wrong, he had approached the Australians at Southerton's Hotel, where Spofforth had gone to practise on his own, with just a couple of men for company. The Demon's look and his furiously fast bowling made me think that an approach to him to compromise his performance would have been met with a livid gaze, seething and scorching enough to turn the interior of any mortal man to jelly.

There was a good deal of cheering as Ulyett blocked the next ball and managed to save his wicket. The spectators by now feared the worst from every ball that this extraordinary bowler bowled, and even the usually unnoteworthy act of keeping it out brought forth plenty of 'bravo' and 'well played'. Despite my mind being occupied with the curious problems with which we had been grappling since the warnings of the previous day, I somehow managed to realise that Spofforth had bowled his four deliveries of the over to four different batsmen. That must have been a rare occurrence, although I am sure my elderly companion in the club room could rattle off an account of such feats by several forgotten Surrey bowlers.

The Oval crowd now had something to cheer about. Garrett was bowling from the Pavilion End, and Grace drove him hard to the on-side, and by the time young Sammy Jones had darted around to cut it off a yard in front of the wall of spectators who stood on the embankment, the batsmen had run three amidst great and raucous cheers from around the ground.

As the field changed over for the next over, my thoughts turned to Holmes, and I wondered about the specific way he would be conducting his enquiries. Perhaps no one else could have found the connection between this apparently random death and the mysterious note that Charles Alcock had received the day before. Yet, once the connection had been established, it was almost impossible to attribute it to mere coincidence. The more I thought about it, the more it seemed to me that the two must be related by some thread which had remained invisible thus far.

I must confess that there was hardly scope for my mind, now thoroughly caught up in the fascinating match being played out, to dwell any further on the matter. There could be no battle in cricket more intriguing than our Champion facing The Demon. Spofforth, all arms, legs and nose, came off his diabolical nine paces, a Catherine wheel of action, a human octopus as he released the ball in a whirl; and at the other end was the mighty batsman, the leviathan, the greatest Champion, with his huge frame and imposing beard, negotiating the deliveries with a judicious mix of forward and back play.

The third ball of the over was driven high on the on-side, but beyond the reach of fielders. By the time it was retrieved and returned, the batsmen had run two. England had reached 20.

There was a quiet interlude now as Ulyett played out a maiden off Garrett, and then the mighty battle was resumed.

Spofforth sent down his delivery with all the venom he could muster, and Grace drove him hard to the on-side. Horan sprinted in hot pursuit, as it made its way to the north-western embankments. It was hard to tell whether the force of Dr Grace's bat would have propelled it over the boundary, or Tom Horan's desperate strides would overtake the ball first. We will never know, for at that moment an urchin jumped from amongst the crowd of standing spectators and grabbed the ball, returning it to the baffled fielder. Four runs were awarded by the umpire, but I feel sure the Australians were not really amused by the incident.

Two balls later, the Doctor drove Spofforth again, and again Horan gave chase; this time he stopped it inside the perimeter, but the batsmen crossed over thrice. The Champion was on his way, paving the path for victory.

There was a knock on the door and Sherlock Holmes re-entered the committee room, accompanied by a youth who looked distinctly out of place in the pavilion, appearing by all aspects to be a groom or handyman. Holmes had a sovereign sticking out of his fist, and seemed intent on keeping it in constant view. The young lad, for his part, entered the room with a deferential bow but his eyes never left the sovereign as he stood there.

"Now, my good lad," Holmes said as he sat with his legs stretched out in front of him, his fist raised in front of his chest with the coin in full view. "Repeat what you saw to me and this gentleman here, and this money is yours."

The eyes of the boy gleamed in expectation. "Say, guv'nor, I hate to be a nose. But Mr Alcock did say you'se not a copper."

"I am not, I can tell you that. I am generally considered the last court of appeal."

This seemed to confuse the boy, but a couple of tosses of the coin in the hand of my friend did away with whatever inhibitions he might have been suffering.

"As I said, guv'nor, I work for Mr Tunewall in his bar. Before the break for lunch we carry supplies from the gates to the bar. I spotted them there, behind them wooden stands, two toffs and a darkie."

"Darkie?"

"Yes, guv'nor, and a crazy one. Looked a proper lascar. I told Mr Tunewall as much, and he laughed and said I had a drink too early. No lascars here. Them niggers were here years earlier, he tells me, to play cricket at this ground, when he was my age. They were also from Australia. But not these Australians we have now. These are white like us."

"Why do you say the dark man was crazy?"

"He was a wild one. He wore a wrapper, a dirty one like a blanket, all the way to his kecks. They stood there arguing. One of the toffs had turned to go when this darkie grabs the other's umbrella and pulls him back, hooking his collar this way. I think to myself how such a darkie got in, a dirty, wild one at that, keen on jolly. I think the toff needs help, but the other swell waves me away. I think about the blueboots, guv'nor, but am never a nose. Am I in trouble, guv'nor?"

"Not in the least. You have made yourself some money. Can you remember where this took place, lad? If it is the right one, I shall hand this over to you."

The boy broke into a smile. "Can do that, guv'nor. 'Twas right next to the stacks of unused wood from the workmen who put up the new stands. A quiet part. Can show you."

There was a murmur around the ground as Spofforth, having bowled a maiden to Ulyett, came on for the next over as well, now with his back to us. Grace drove him through the off-side and amidst great cheers the batsmen took two.

Holmes was at my shoulder, as the boy waited outside. "Watson, we do make progress and make it fast. It must have struck you that our young friend here was talking of the dead man."

I looked at my friend in some surprise. "Holmes, in this huge, huge crowd, how in God's name did you find the eyewitness?"

Holmes laughed at my bewildered expression. "There is a delightful freshness about you, Watson, which makes it a pleasure to exercise any small powers which I possess at your expense. But it is simplicity itself. The man had a meeting scheduled at one in the afternoon, and I was quite certain something unusual had taken place during the course of this encounter. Not only did the man complain of chest pain after this, he also became a trifle sketchy and careless when it came to jotting down in his scorebook the details of what went on in the field. Since he could not very well go onto the field to meet whoever it was, there was just one place for him. Behind the wooden stands. With the match at such an interesting juncture, there was not too high a probability of the rear of the stands being frequented by many people. Yet, chances were high that any unusual activity would draw attention. But whose? Who moves around the rear of the ground when all others are busy watching the game? The answer is simple, the men who come here not to watch the game but to perform their daily jobs. Mr Tunewall is in charge of the refreshment bar behind the stands. There is also the Tavern run by Ind Coope and Company, but that is on the far side of the ground. I assembled all the helping hands who load, unload, wash and clean for Mr Tunewall and asked whether any of them had seen anything unusual. I offered a shilling at first, and a couple of men came up airing figments of their imagination, cock-and-bull stories, but this lad was telling the truth. The description he gave of his 'toff' matched our poor departed friend. I wanted to make sure of certain aspects of his tale, and made him repeat it to you. Now, Watson, I think we are about to have the full set of facts in our hands. I will allow you to get back to the game. As ever, keep watching out for unusual activity."

As Holmes walked out, I wondered if I should go with him. Yet, he had himself emphasised that it was important to stay focused on the game. As usual, he had fascinated me with his cold stream of logic cutting through the mystery in this amphitheatre that was now hotting up with extreme tension. It was also evident to me that he was intent on using the committee room as his consulting office at the ground and it was important that I remain there. I confess I was concocting various justifications for my staying put, in order to follow the course of the game. When Grace struck Boyle high and handsomely to the legside boundary, I no longer felt apologetic about leaving my friend to his own devices.

Ulyett was also starting to bat effectively, the excellent all-rounder that he was. Spofforth continued in his tireless efforts, but now the Yorkshireman struck him convincingly to square leg for four. The cheering was thunderous. The next ball was driven hard and high, but it was stopped at long off and only a solitary run was taken. Grace faced Spofforth again in another titanic struggle within the great game, and our greatest batsman cut the ball away and ran up and down twice.

If the cheers had been tremendous till then, they became thunderous when Grace struck Spofforth firmly to the onside and ran two to bring up the 50 of the innings. Only 35 were needed to win. Ulyett was playing, if not very well, very freely, and Grace was carefully constructing a masterpiece of an innings. Even The Demon, who had often got the better of our Champion, had not managed to get a ball past his bat. All those who remained ready to go in down the order were first-class batsmen, every one of them except Peate. It was probably going to be too easy, and I wondered again whether I should have been out there with Holmes, lending him a hand.

The thought did not have much of an opportunity to grow in the weak soil of my mind. Spofforth was running in at a furious pace and testing Ulyett to his limits. He managed to play the first ball of the over safely, but the next one was almost unplayable. The furious delivery touched the edge of his bat, and Blackham, that great wicketkeeper, caught him fast and low to his right. It was the grandest bowling, a superlative act of athleticism, and Ulyett walked back with a morose expression on his face. The half hour Grace and Ulyett had been together had almost decided the game, but still 34 needed to be made. Bunny Lucas, the Cambridge University man who had turned from hero to villain by spilling Massie's catch in the morning, now entered the fray, with another grand opportunity to emerge a hero.

The reassuring presence of Grace at the other end soothed the nerves of the electrified crowd. Boyle ran in to bowl his right-arm medium pace, and was cut away for two. 32 were required and, with enough assistance from his fellow men, Grace could get them alone. The bowler delivered his next ball and the giant played it cautiously. The Doctor looked determined to be there till the end. I wondered for a while what my elderly friend in the club room was thinking, and into whose ear he was pouring his observations now that I was no longer there.

Boyle turned again and ran in to bowl to Grace, pitching it up, inviting a drive. Grace put his front foot down the wicket and drove hard. Alas, the ball dipped just short of a half-volley and WG did not get hold of it. The ball gained height, travelling straight to Alick Bannerman at mid-off. In the shocked silence that followed, one could almost hear the sound of a thousand English hearts breaking in unison. The heavily bearded Boyle had got the prize wicket of WG Grace, the most famous beard in the world. England were 53 for 4.

CHAPTER 11

SPOFFORTH AND BOYLE

THE advantage of a few minutes earlier had been comprehensively neutralised. With Grace back in the pavilion, it was anyone's game now. Our wicketkeeper Lyttelton, a capital batsman in his own right, was trotting out to join Lucas at the wicket.

For the next few minutes the game felt so precarious, such a strain on the nerves, that I wondered if our dead man would have managed to survive them with his weak heart even if he had not been assaulted during the clandestine meeting. The atmosphere was almost too tense to bear for even the healthiest of men. Spofforth bowled with every bit of devilry, and Lyttelton, with absolutely no idea what he was doing, managed to snick one behind the stumps for three. The Almighty alone knows how it missed the bails on its way. Every ball was now being watched with extreme anxiety. Spofforth and Boyle resembled the two horns of the devil, with Lucas and Lyttelton only just managing to survive their guile.

In the midst of all this, one of Spofforth's devious deliveries kicked up and took the glove of Lucas, falling just beyond the outstretched hand of Murdoch at point.

At the stroke of five o'clock, Lyttelton struck Spofforth and found the middle of the bat. The ball travelled fast and, despite the Australian fielders metamorphosing into greyhounds, made it to the boundary. This seemed to break a dam of tension and restraint. The crowd roared their applause, cheering vociferously as a run came off the next ball too. There were just 20 to score. Surely England could not lose from this situation.

Yet, I was apprehensive. Spofforth and Boyle were untiring, making the balls rear, bounce and break from a perfect length. The fielders, led by the sprightly Bannerman, were like a moving human barricade through which no ball could pass.

Then began a phase in which over after over was sent down, every ball witnessed at the cost of cracked knuckles and bitten nails, while not a run was scored. Boyle was bowling to Lyttelton and Spofforth to Lucas. And that way they seemed destined to stay, the action painted on the canvas of eternity. I glanced at the clock and it told me fifteen minutes had passed without a run being scored. My pulse raced as I sat sweating, even though cold gusts were blowing in through a crack in the window pane.

I heard a knock and suddenly remembered that Holmes was out there, investigating a crime whose nature was as yet uncertain. I had all but forgotten about the purpose of our visit to the pavilion, and sprang up from my chair with hasty steps to open the door, crying, "Holmes, where have you been?"

The man who entered, however, was not Holmes. It was a cricketer, his flannels and pads just about visible under an enormous blanket he had wrapped around himself. The man was shivering violently.

The tale told by the refreshment bar attendant flashed through my mind. The man in the blanket! But this person was not a 'darkie' as the colourful language of the helping hand had described the assailant with the umbrella. He was a very young, very sober and almost ascetic looking England cricketer; he did not look a day older than two-and-twenty. A closer look revealed his identity and I exclaimed, "Why, I have the pleasure of meeting Charlie Studd! I thought you should have been in there by now."

The young man was too tense to speak coherently. "Hornby said he would be changing the order. Wants to hold me in reserve. Mind if I sit here, sir? It's awfully cold."

He was shivering uncontrollably, and I focused my physician's eye on him. There were some tropical diseases I had encountered in Afghanistan and India which resulted in such symptoms. But it was soon evident to me that all that young CT Studd was suffering from was a bad case of nerves.

"By all means, you can sit here, sir. But, what if Hornby wants you to bat?"

"He knows I am in the committee room, and I think he will be sending Steel in next. But, sir, the match seems to be stuck in a stalemate as in a chess game. Nothing has happened for perhaps an hour or more."

I looked at my watch. "They have gone twenty minutes without a run or a wicket. Seems like an eternity."

"It grows dark, sir." Studd spoke no more. He sat there, and his knees knocked against each other, such was the extent of his tension. Indeed, the skies were gloomy; soon it would be very difficult to see the ball.

"Don't worry, young man, I'm sure you'll come back a hero today," I said as Spofforth completed yet another maiden over to Lucas.

Studd looked at me with dreamy eyes. "Thank you. That is kind, sir, but… what is all the fame and flattery worth? Over after over, it remains, like eternity, as you so wisely said. What is it worth a win when a man comes face to face with eternity?"

It seemed to me that the tension had gone to his head, but there was a certain earnestness in his speech that made me wonder whether there was more to it.

"Vanity of vanities, all is vanity," he concluded.

Out in the middle Lyttleton pushed Boyle to the leg side and after the 'eternity' there was a run. Bannerman of all people fumbled and let it through and the batsmen crossed over.

"Did you see that, sir?" I remarked in great excitement. "Alick Bannerman of all people mis-fielding that docile push. Cheer up, CT. It is eternity no more."

The young man's voice shook as he answered. "I saw Spofforth speak to Bannerman before the over, sir. I am sure that was contrived. Spofforth wants to bowl to Lyttelton, because he has not played him with anything approaching confidence. Oh, sir, I can't bear to watch. The deceitful ploy! Poor Lyttelton cannot change ends without taking risks. The bowlers are extremely accurate and there are fielders everywhere. The Australians don't have a long stop, sir, Blackham doesn't need one. By all considerations they have a fielder more."

"But a sudden miss on Blackham's part can get us valuable runs."

"Blackham does not miss them, sir."

We watched Lyttelton somehow negotiate another over from Spofforth, when there were a couple of loud raps on the door. My new companion winced.

"Do you expect company here, sir? Sorry to have entered uninvited, I will look for some other sanctuary where there is peace."

He got up from his chair and wrapped his blanket around him. The door opened and Holmes came in, with Mr Alcock and a nervous looking man of some forty years of age.

"Studd?" Alcock exclaimed. "What on earth are you doing here when you may be needed at any time? What's that thing you have around you?"

"I do hope, sir, I'll be able to deliver when the call comes," the young man said, rather morose.

"Buck up, lad, there is a game to win."

"I'll do my best, sir."

He was about to leave when Holmes laid a hand on his shoulder.

"Excuse me, Mr Studd, but can you tell me where you found the blanket?"

Studd looked vaguely into my friend's eyes. "I found it lying in the pavilion. I put it on because I was shivering with cold."

"Do you know whose it is?"

Studd shook his head. "It is hard in a spirit of honesty to accept something found as a free gift, but I thanked the Lord for his remarkable kindness. I was feeling so cold. I will leave it where I found it when I have to go out... Oh... my God... You see, sir, I was afraid of this...."

There was good reason for his consternation. At that moment Lyttelton had missed a ball from Spofforth, and it struck the top of his middle stump. Studd left the room in haste. Alcock raised his arms in frustration.

"66 for 5. I cannot help wondering why Hornby changed the batting order."

"I would not have, sir," came the apologetic voice of the other man in the room. "I would have sent Mr Studd ahead of Lyttleton."

Holmes turned towards the speaker, eyes gleaming in his sharp features.

"I have no doubt we would be most interested in your opinions on the batting order, but we have more pressing matters to take care of at present. Watson, I don't know whether it falls within your sphere of expertise or not, but could you tell me if tension causes men to chew something other than their fingernails?"

Familiar though I am with my friend's methods, this particular question was so unexpected that I was temporarily speechless.

"Meet Mr Arthur Courcy of Epsom, whose trade I believe is bookmaking. I see that's a Pink 'un sticking out of your pocket."

Mr Courcy replied in a steady voice, "There is nothing illegal in my business, Mr Holmes."

"That may be put to the test if we have sufficient time and inclination. What I'd really like to know is why you chewed clean through the handle of your umbrella."

The man replied in a shaky voice, "I have told you, sir, the tension is unbearable. It makes one do strange things. You just saw what it has done to Mr Studd now, talking like a fruitcake and his teeth are chattering. On the way here we met Mr Barnes downstairs. And I can tell you his teeth would have chattered as well, had he not left them at home."

On the field Allan Steel had joined Lucas. However, my attention was now on Courcy and the mangled umbrella Holmes held in his hand.

"It is extremely unlikely that one would be driven to chew the handle of an umbrella, sir, and deform it in that way," I remarked.

"It is an unusual match, sir, and we do strange things."

"And why is it, man, that you shake so whenever we speak of the umbrella?" It was Mr Alcock who asked the question.

"Why, sir, I am a husband and a father, and this is my brother-in-law's umbrella. My missus dotes on her brother, and when I return it to him, I will hear no end of it. Any of you a married man, sirs?"

Holmes laughed in excellent humour. "You are a rather curious man, Mr Courcy. Fear and tension affects you in very odd ways. The match makes you chew the handle of your umbrella while I can see every nail of your hand is impeccably intact. And then when the umbrella itself is mentioned you shake like a leaf out of fear of your wife."

"My wife always had that effect on me, sir. So does cricket. Friends tell me that the game is my mistress."

"You have a remarkable sense of humour, I have to admit, sir, though it will be my conjecture that it is the shield that you employ against fear." Holmes laughed. He had to delay his exposition because at this moment Steel leaned forward to a ball that came in slower and spooned a catch back to Spofforth and no one was quite focused on what the great detective had to say.

"Heavens, what a wretched stroke to play at this time," Alcock exclaimed. "We are six wickets down. How many do we have to get?"

"Sixteen, sir," replied Courcy.

"Fifteen, the score is 70," I corrected him.

Holmes clapped his hands. "Splendid. Now that we have settled the issue of the score, perhaps we can concentrate on the matter at hand. Your jovial stories about your umbrella, your wife and your brother-in-law are most amusing. But it does seem stretching the boundaries of probability a bit too far to find you sitting in the same stand, just a few feet away from the dead man."

"It's Read, and still no sign of Studd," exclaimed Mr Alcock as the new England batsman made his way to the wicket. "My apologies, Mr Holmes, but I find Hornby's tactics too strange for words. Please carry on."

Holmes raised the umbrella and peered at it. "It is an unusually fine handle, and the varnish has preserved its fashionable light colour. If you don't have two sets of teeth, Mr Courcy, and I assume the excitement of the match has not made you grow a second set, it would have taken you at least an hour or even more to gnaw through the entire thing in this manner. Since I apprehended you before the series of maiden overs were bowled, when tension was at its peak, you must have started your tooth-work much, much earlier. For some reason, you were intent on disfiguring the handle almost as soon as the England innings started. Why was that, Mr Courcy? Was it because you had seen me in the stands and knew my reputation? Quite a few of your trade do know me by name and by sight. Was it because you wanted to leave no trace of blood on the wood?"

The suggestions made by Holmes in this monologue were so striking that Mr Alcock hardly reacted when Spofforth's ball broke in to hit Read's middle and off stumps.

In spite of his efforts at jocularity, Courcy had turned a little pale. "Why would there be blood on the wood, Mr Holmes? The man, we all know, died of a heart condition. He was also undone by the tension in the game. This is no place for weak hearts."

"My dear Mr Courcy, you will be delighted to know that Doctor WG Grace himself agrees with this particular sentiment."

Mr Alcock struggled to suppress the signs of frustration he felt as he saw Barnes walking out to bat ahead of Studd. He did not utter a word about it, and even for me it was too baffling to explain. Courcy looked at the ground and exclaimed, "Barnes! Well, gosh-all my fishhooks …"

"Never mind Barnes, Mr Courcy. Perhaps Hornby went for someone whose teeth would not chatter. Now, what if I say I can produce someone who recognises you as one of the men who had been talking to the dead man at one o'clock? It was your umbrella that was grabbed and used to assault the man, wasn't it?"

At last Blackham did make an error. Spofforth's ball was too fast and too low and he missed it. The grateful English batsmen ran three byes.

Mr Alcock was too focused on Holmes' exposition to even rejoice at that stroke of good fortune. As for Courcy, he was shivering just as much as Studd had been. The colour had drained from his face. He reached out a shaky hand and grabbed a chair, lowering his quivering form into it.

"It's no use denying it, sir, but it was not a blow. Just an attempt to stop him from walking away. The gentleman tried to catch his collar with my umbrella, and the cussed fella turned at an unhappy moment. The brolly struck him on his head, and there was blood. He looked at us with frightened eyes and walked away. We were trying to reason with him, Mr Holmes, not to bring his brand of villainy into the game. I may be a bookmaker, sir, but an honest one. I know the two words sound funny when taken together, but I don't fix the results or manipulate them as Spenlow was trying to do."

"His name's Spenlow?"

"Yes, sir, it is. Look up his record and it is long as my arm. He had been busy trying to get in touch with the Australian players. And he was intent on getting my bookmaking trade under his control to promote his nexus."

A groan coursed through the ground. Lucas, having taken his time to look around the field before facing

Spofforth, aimed for glory with a preconceived stroke and played on. The batsman was so annoyed with himself that he lifted his bat and struck the dead ball. In spite of the surprising revelations that had confronted us during the last few minutes, Alcock clutched his forehead.

"We're done for. Now if Peate is sent in ahead of Studd, I will have to certify Hornby as a lunatic."

Courcy was now too agitated to turn his attention to the game. Holmes waited for him to continue, as I stole a glance through the window to see Studd walking out at long last, thankfully without his blanket.

"Who was the Australian gentleman with you who used the umbrella on Spenlow?"

Courcy looked up with his eyes a strange mixture of fear and unflinching resolve.

"I can't say that, Mr Holmes. You can put me in prison, you can indeed send me to the gallows. But there is honour amongst the likes of us. The gentleman will remain unnamed."

"God bless my soul," exclaimed Mr Alcock with intense passion. Out in the field, Boyle had sent one kicking up at Barnes, and the batsman had gloved it. The Australian captain, creeping in closer and closer, grasped the catch at point.

The ninth England wicket was down.

"I'm sorry, Mr Holmes, but I'm beside myself. You must really forgive me, but as long as I have played cricket, I never can sit and watch the game in silence," exclaimed Mr Alcock. "Hornby apparently said that he was keeping Studd up his sleeve. And now up in the sleeve he will remain forever. Here comes Peate, and every run he scores will be a bonus."

At this moment a curious occurrence left even Holmes with an expression of confusion that one does not normally associate with him. As poor Ted Peate, his moustache drooping lower than usual, made the long, long journey to the wicket, Courcy got up from his seat, rejuvenated, and walked over to a chair right in front of the window.

"Gentlemen, by your leave, before I am hauled away to the gallows, jailed, hung until death for eating an umbrella… whatever you choose to do with me, before that I would like to watch my last bit of cricket from the Oval pavilion."

I looked at Holmes, and then at Charles Alcock. I can write in all honesty that, though the Surrey secretary was struggling with the heinous secrets and accidental death on one hand and the colossal failure of the England batting on the other, at these words from the bookmaker his face glowed with something akin to paternal pride.

Holmes, undecided for a moment or two, suddenly burst out laughing and joined us at the window. "It would be positively cruel of me if I kept you gentlemen from enjoying the last bit of this crazy game of yours by making you listen to my precise logical arguments. Go ahead, Mr Alcock, and you too, Watson. Let's see what happens now."

We all moved to the window. Boyle, ball in hand, waited as the slow left-arm bowler from Yorkshire took his guard. Tall and stooping, without a semblance of athleticism, Peate stood in his left-handed stance to face the bowling.

His instructions were probably explicit. Block. Give Studd the chance of getting the runs. Studd, I may add, had not yet faced a single delivery.

Boyle ran in, and Peate hoicked him with a curious agricultural manner, sending the ball into the outfield behind square leg. The batsmen ran once, and almost as an afterthought ran again. Garrett fielded the ball and sent in the return. Umpire Luke Greenwood, standing at square leg, threw himself on his stomach, perhaps to avoid the throw from decapitating him, but ostensibly to see whether the England number eleven had reached his end and grounded his bat.

Mr Alcock was beside himself in agitation. "What in God's name is Peate doing?"

"Why, sir?" said I. "Two runs are two runs. Eight more needed."

"Well, it will be of use only if he doesn't want to get more. It is dark and Peate is dreadfully short-sighted."

"I know the feeling," intoned our curious companion Courcy, adding in a rather contrived hashed metaphor. "Make hay before the axe drops."

"If Peate survives the next two balls, sir, I will eat my shirt," Mr Alcock exploded.

"If he does, sir, I will supply the gravy," added Courcy.

"Heaven knows why Studd took the second run."

"Well, you heard him talk as well as I. He has turned into a fruitcake," was the astute analysis of Courcy.

I marvelled at the man's indefatigable, macabre humour. Sherlock Holmes sat observing us all, his keen eyes displaying a look that told me that he found such fascination for sport over life, death and gallows quite beyond the realms of reason, but irresistibly hilarious.

Boyle ran in again, and bowled the third ball of the over. Peate waved his bat, trying a shot that made sense only in a book of batsmanship penned by his own hand. Blackham collected it behind the stumps. The entire ground sighed in momentary relief.

It was twelve minutes to six when Boyle began his run for the final ball of the over. It came through straight and on target. Peate swung across the line, in the archetypal manner of a man who felt his job was over when he had bowled his last. The ball went ahead, undeterred and unchallenged, and crashed into the stumps.

There was deathly silence, and a sharp intake of breath from Alcock He sat down on a huge iron safe that was in the room, buried his face in his hands, and remained oblivious to everything.

Then the ground erupted in a great, great yell. The Australians had won one of the greatest cricket matches ever played, by a thin margin of seven runs. The crowd, which had behaved impeccably till now, broke through onto the field and soon the Australian cricketers were being shaken by the hand and slapped on the back. Spofforth and Boyle were chaired on the shoulders of spectators all the way to the pavilion. A steward stood at the gate, and we watched in greatest mirth as he was flung head over heels by a well-dressed gentleman who rushed out to congratulate the fielding team.

Sherlock Holmes now spoke. "Mr Alcock, is that gentleman there Mr Charles Beal?" He was pointing to the very man who had knocked over the attendant in his incredible display of joy.

"Yes, sir, he is. The manager of the Australian team, a lawyer in Melbourne."

"Ah. Could you please send word for him to come up to this room? I promise you, this is the last piece of the puzzle."

Mr Alcock stood there undecided, looking horrified at the very suggestion.

"Mr Holmes, this is the greatest moment after a great match when all the members of both the teams will be expected to celebrate the occasion. We honestly cannot…"

"Do as the gent says, sir." It was Courcy who spoke. "I don't know how he does it, but he knows everything."

Burdened by infinite misgivings Mr Alcock opened the door and stepped outside. As he did so, the familiar high-pitched voice of our Champion floated in, "I left six men to score 30-odd runs, sir…"

CHAPTER 12

SHERLOCK HOLMES HOLDS COURT

OUTSIDE CONFINES of the committee room where we sat, the main club premises were in a shimmering frenzy of excitement. Cheers were given by both teams, in the spirit of camaraderie that graces an occasion when two splendidly spirited and well matched sides play a game of sterling quality.

On the ground, a most vocal multitude was swarming all over the field, their raised voices demanding the appearance of Spofforth, of Murdoch, of Boyle, of Massie, and several even called for Grace.

It was as if the severe tension of the day had been released in a flow of mingling brotherhood and bonhomie. Yet there was no abating of the nervous suspense that engulfed the few of us in seclusion behind closed doors. Charles Alcock sat on the iron safe, his lips pursed in anxiety. Courcy looked out of the window in a vacant gaze, seeming to have resigned himself to an uncertain and unbecoming future. We were waiting for Charlie Beal, the man we had seen rejoicing with such emphatic expressions of joy at the Australian win.

I myself was torn between the cruel horns of dilemma. On the one hand there was my insatiable desire to be abreast of the truth that lay behind the mysterious events, a trait that had grown in the past year of association with my friend. On the other hand I wanted to give in to the surge of excitement that was pulsing through my veins, the surge that had been rising throughout the day, driven by this king of all games. Besides, due to some peculiar human weakness, a part of me wanted to be next to the venerable gentleman of the early part of the day who had foretold the certainty of the Colonials being crushed by the mighty English power and whose prophecies had by now surely come back to haunt him.

Mr Alcock could contain himself no longer. "Mr Holmes, are you sure that involving a person as important as Mr Charles Beal is necessary under the circumstances? I need not repeat that there are many delicate threads that may become irrevocably tangled…You must realise that, as the secretary of this club, there are a number of things that I have to attend to at close of play."

My friend stood there. The persona of clear reason refused to be disturbed by the ripples of excitement that coursed through the entire Oval.

"A man is dead, Mr Alcock. There is a separate thread of murky dealings that run through the entire day. We are most fortunate that it was not able to penetrate the game itself…"

"No, it didn't." Courcy seemed a man incapable of remaining silent in spite of the most damning of circumstances. "If it had been, then the odds after Massie's innings would have been deliberately shortened, for England and Australia would have stumbled at the end."

"Aha," Holmes cried. "That is more or less what I had surmised. Now, Mr Alcock, some small details of this day still need to be cleared up. Truth is better than endless doubt. Humour me this final time. When this gentleman comes in, ask him for a cigarette."

"I beg your pardon, Mr Holmes?"

"Come on, sir, tell him the last few minutes of the match have been a test for your nerves, and you have run out of your own cigarettes."

"But…"

"Watson, now that the match is over, you can perhaps do something for me. Stand in front of our friend Mr Courcy here so that he is not immediately visible when Mr Beal comes through the door."

There was a knock on the door and a jubilant gentleman entered the room. Charlie Beal was in the prime of life, a well-tailored black coat and top hat lending a certain aura to his person, the well-groomed moustache adding to the effect. But it was the victorious smile splitting his face from ear to ear that struck us as he walked in.

"You rang for me, Sir Alcock?" he asked in mock deference, bowling slightly. "Better make this extra quick, my vanquished friend. Hornby has just passed around glasses of champagne, seltzer and lemon, and I can do with quite a few gulps after today. Everyone is gay! Why, my mother took young Giffen in her arms and planted a kiss on his cheeks as if embracing a newborn."

In keeping with the élan with which he carried out his multiple responsibilities, Mr Alcock rose to the occasion. "Yes, Mr Beal. But, before that, my friends and I are dying for a smoke. And I am out of cigars. I've smoked them all through the last couple of hours. Can you lend me a cigarette?"

Mr Beal laughed loudly and fished in his pockets. A smidgeon of red in his cheeks told me that he had partaken of Hornby's delicious cocktail already.

"Certainly, the least I can do to cheer you up after what Spofforth did to you..."

"Could we have one of the *Kyriazi Frères*? I have a partiality for the Egyptian brand of tobacco." It was Holmes who spoke, in a tone that merged to perfection with the air of geniality flowing around so that none of us realized anything was out of the ordinary.

"Well, they are precious ones," laughed Mr Beal. "But, since you ask... but, sir, how did you come to know of the Egyptian cigarettes?"

Sherlock Holmes produced a small cloth bundle and proceeded to untie it before laying the contents on the table in front of us. I peered from where I stood and saw a small scattering of cigarette ash.

"Watson, if you would be so kind as to close the door, it would be advisable for all of us."

As I walked towards the door, Mr Beal's expression changed into one of unpleasant surprise. "What's going on, Mr Alcock? What are we doing here? Why are you not outside, celebrating with the cricketers…" He broke off as his gaze fell on Courcy, who now sat in open view since I had left my post to close the door. His voice quivered. "Courcy? What are you doing here? Why is this man here? What's going on? Look here, Mr Alcock, I am a lawyer and I won't stand for this."

Holmes stepped forward and pointed to the remnants of smoked tobacco.

"I wonder, Mr Beal, whether your educational pursuits on your way to becoming a lawyer allowed you to dabble in the peripheral topics that lend so much accuracy to the science of criminal investigations. As Watson here will testify, I have devoted my attention to the topic of tobacco ash, and have written a little monograph on the ashes of 140 different varieties of pipe, cigar and cigarette tobacco. When I discovered this ash at the scene where you, Mr Beal, had your unpleasant little rendezvous today, I could determine the cigarette smoked was as one of the excellent brand of Cairo's *Kyriazi Frères.*"

Mr Beal stood there with a frown, his expression oscillating between anger and uncertainty.

"What rendezvous? Here, Courcy, what stories have you been telling these gentlemen? Mr Alcock, this is most unacceptable. Who are these men here?"

Holmes proceeded with a calm, clear voice. "You do our friend Mr Courcy grave injustice, Mr Beal. He has not mentioned your name even once, in spite of our pointed enquiries in that regard. As for myself, I am Sherlock Holmes, consulting detective, and have been engaged by Mr Charles Alcock to investigate the misdemeanours that were hinted at in the letter of warning he received yesterday. I believe, Mr Beal, that as the writer of that letter you have been instrumental in bringing me into the matter."

Mr Alcock now asked in a rather confused voice, "Mr Beal, was it you who sent the letter?"

"Yes, indeed Mr Beal wrote it at the Southerton Hotel and delivered it to the pavilion. I am sure he had the best intentions, acting for the sake of the game, what with the late Mr Spenlow dogging the footsteps of the Australian cricketers …"

"That villain Spenlow!" Mr Beal exploded. "Yes, he was following my men all around. Trying to get in touch with Murdoch, Boyle and Spoff. That goes to show you that the bookmaking racket is as prevalent here as in Australia, no matter what you write in your periodical, Mr Alcock."

Holmes flicked a brief glance at our client. "It indeed is, my dear sir."

Mr Beal continued. "I tell you, sir, I did have strong words with him and I don't regret having said them. He tried Courcy here to rig the bets for him, only our man here has his principles and he tried to reason with him. But Spenlow would not listen …" He broke off as he realized the implications of what Holmes had said. "Did you say late Mr Spenlow, Mr Holmes? Is he dead?"

"Indeed he is." Sherlock Holmes clapped his hands as if in glee. "And from your expression, sir, I know now that this is news to you."

Charles Beal cried with emotion. "You can say that, sir. It is a surprise, and I will be tempting the wrath of God if I don't speak the unadulterated truth and let it be known that the surprise is in many ways a pleasant one. This Spenlow, gentlemen, was a conniving villain, heaven have mercy on his soul. If such men are allowed to walk free in the world, the great game as we know it will soon be reduced to a conduit for ill-gotten gains. I did hear someone had fallen dead while watching the match. Was that Spenlow?"

"It was, Mr Beal," Mr Alcock said in a hoarse voice. "Pardon me, gentlemen, but this string of revelations has tried my faculties to the limit. Mr Holmes, as you see, Mr Beal here was not even aware that the man was dead."

"I do see that, Mr Alcock."

"Could you please tell me how the Egyptian cigarettes come into the scheme of things?"

Holmes turned his gaze towards me. "Surely, Watson, having been good enough to draw up some accounts of the cases I have been involved in, and even occasionally embellishing them, you will be able to settle this trivial issue for the gentlemen here?"

I had so many reasons to believe in my friend's absolute powers of reasoning that I felt he must have some solid grounds for the assured and easy demeanour with which he treated this singularly puzzling mystery. Yet, for the life of me, I could not make out how the cigarette had any bearing on the case.

Holmes looked most disappointed when I drew a blank.

"Pardon my rudeness, gentlemen, but I seldom have time for trivialities. However, since you ask .... According to the documents provided by Mr Alcock, I could ascertain that the Australian contingent sailed on the *Assam,* and made their way via Galle in Ceylon, the straits of Babelmandep, the island of Perim, into the Red Sea, giving Aden a wide berth and docking at Port Said. After that they passed through Malta and on to Plymouth, where Mr Beal and three other men disembarked, while the rest sailed to the London docks. The adventurous smokers among the party were not averse to stocking up their collections of tobacco, cigarettes and pipes at the various halts along the way. When I discovered this particular variety of ash at the place where, according to one of Mr Tunewall's barhands, Mr Beal, Mr Courcy and Spenlow had a conference, I could deduce that this had been left by one of the Australian party. The cigarettes must have been purchased the cigarettes at Port Said, or have been presented by the British soldiers posted there. Spenlow did not have any such cigarette on his person, nor does Courcy, who smokes the Phillip Morris Oxford Blues."

"But, how did you know it was me if Courcy did not divulge my name?"

Holmes looked at me once again, his probing eyes holding an enquiring look.

"Watson, while CT Studd was sitting here before he went out to bat, did you get a close look at the blanket?"

I reflected on the frayed old thing that the young batsman had wrapped around himself. It was a plain old white blanket, with some smudges due to overuse.

"As always, Watson, I should point out the difference between seeing and observing. The smudges that you saw were not merely smudges. One in particular had been a bad reproduction of the eagle Aquila, the standard symbol of a Roman legion. There had been attempts to wash it out, but the amateurish marks were permanent enough to allow us to decipher the original crude paintwork. If I am not mistaken, the blanket belongs to Mr George Bonnor, and was used by him to masquerade as a Roman soldier in the fancy dress ball on the *Assam*. It was not a memorable performance if accounts we have heard are true, but the blanket is perhaps something that accompanies Bonnor in his cricket bag for reasons best known to him. The question is, how did Mr Studd get hold of the blanket? He told us something to the effect that it had been lying in the pavilion. It had obviously been left there after being used by someone who had access to the Australian dressing room."

Holmes looked closely at Mr Beal, who was listening with rapt attention and with something akin to awe on his face.

"It was obviously difficult for a member of the Australian party to meet a man notoriously linked with the bookmaking profession on the premises of The Oval during an important match. It would be even more difficult if the member is the manager of the Australian team. Hence, Mr Beal, you decided to meet him in disguise. In your mind, which was perhaps feverish, running over with extreme rage at the continuous contacts made by Spenlow with his unethical demands, you had to make the best of whatever resources were available to you. You remembered the ship-board parties, and decided to use Bonnor's blanket to conceal yourself. Additionally, you fell back on the Bones and Tambo act that you had carried out with captain Billy Murdoch. I hear the two of you had given an excellent performance. You burnt a piece of cork and painted your face as black as possible."

"The Lascar!" I exclaimed. "That's why the man from the bar said that the man wrapped in a blanket was a darkie like a Lascar."

"Excellent, Watson. Having put on your disguise, you went ahead to meet the unfortunate Spenlow and got into a heated argument. He disagreed with whatever it was you were saying."

Charles Beal spoke in an excited voice. "Mr Holmes, I am amazed at your ability to deduce the sequence of events from such small bits of evidence. Yes, it happened almost exactly as you say. But why are we discussing this? I did write that letter to Mr Alcock, hoping that he would take some steps to keep nefarious elements like Spenlow out of the ground today. I did everything in my power to stop the villain from contacting the players. Why, he had enraged Spoff to such an extent at Southerton's with his suggestions of compromising his performance that I was not entirely sure that our bowler in chief would not direct his anger uselessly at this vile man rather than focusing on the cricket. I dare say if WG had not carried out that mean trick on young Jones, Spoff would be still thinking of Spenlow and would not have concentrated his anger on England. Spoff can be very difficult to handle sometimes. He was challenged to a duel on the ship by a stupid Frenchman. It came to nothing only because Murdoch, acting as his second, suggested buckets as the weapon of choice. As it is, we have had a great game of cricket where both teams played to their best ability, and played to win. I was apprehensive that Spenlow would make other attempts at influencing the match after I had seen him off, but it seems he had good reason not to … by being dead. All's well that ends well."

"You shouldn't have grabbed my umbrella and struck him, sir," offered Courcy, almost forgotten while our attention was taken up by this striking series of revelations. He was still sitting in the chair in front of the window where he had been ever since his decision to enjoy the last bit of the match. "That you shouldn't have done, sir."

CHAPTER 13

THE ASHES

"OH, REALLY?" Mr Beal fumed. "The man just turned away saying that even if I didn't agree to speak to the players and convey his offer, he would find other ways to do the needful. He wanted to stop the conversation, walk away and get on with his double dealings as Satan's minion. I grabbed Courcy's umbrella and tried to hook him by the neck and swing him around. I did not hit him, he just turned his face and was struck by the handle. What of it, gentlemen? Am I going to be charged with assaulting a seedy rascal with an umbrella?"

There was a pause during which, in spite of the anger, indignation, confusion and a fair amount of champagne that he had imbibed, Mr Charles Beal seemed to hit upon the diabolical truth.

"You don't mean, sir, that my blow with the umbrella — a grazing blow at that — was enough to kill the man? That's absurd, gentlemen. Courcy here knows the way the blow was struck, by accident, and it just scratched the side of his forehead. Come, come, sirs, a man cannot die from that sort of a thing. We cannot be talking of manslaughter here."

Mr Beal had suddenly started to sweat as the enormity of the incident became apparent to him.

Sherlock Holmes spoke now, his voice calm and reassuring in spite of the cold reason that had so far dominated his manner in this dramatic scene.

"We can indeed be talking of manslaughter here. Let me tell you a little tale from my collection of sensational news from around the country. Watson here will vouch for it that I am quite a connoisseur of such morbid trivia. Not too long ago there was a death of an unfortunate lad who ran against a post and died of concussion to the brain. It was proved that the boy had thrown a missile at an elder brother and, to escape punishment, had run away. Whilst looking round to see if his brother were near, he ran into the post with the fatal result. The verdict was manslaughter, because the coroner advised the jury that, as the boy was in bodily fear, the elder brother was criminally responsible for the death. The magistrates refused to convict him, but the man was put on trial at the Assizes and the judge held the coroner was right, and the accused was sentenced to prison. It may interest you to know that this incident took place in East Gloucestershire, and the coroner in question was none other than our friend Dr EM Grace."

There was a sharp intake of breath from Mr Alcock, and Mr Beal looked extremely agitated. Sherlock Holmes continued:

"On this occasion, however, there might be a rather more direct causal connection between the grazing blow by the umbrella that drew blood and the death of the victim. It is perhaps not too difficult to argue that the condition of his weak heart was aggravated by the excitement and by the assault on his person."

"How dreadful, how dreadful," murmured Mr Alcock. "But, Mr Holmes …"

"The most interesting aspect of this incident is that the coroner of our last tale, Dr EM Grace, has already inspected the body, and his assessment is firmly 'death by a weak condition of the heart'. This was my friend Dr Watson's diagnosis as well. I don't know about you, Mr Alcock, but personally I don't see any reason to make alterations to the considered and qualified impressions of these two excellent medical men."

As Holmes stopped speaking, the faces of all three of our companions registered a range of emotions that slowly shifted through a cloud of despondency to confusion to the final silver lining of hope.

"Mr Holmes," Charles Alcock started speaking first. "If I grasp your meaning correctly, it will be of great benefit to the club, to the game, to the country and to the Australians if this unfortunate event…"

"After all, Mr Alcock," said Holmes, reaching in his pocket for his clay pipe. "I am not retained by the police to supply leads and consultation for every death that takes place. If our Mr Beal here were a dangerous criminal, it would have been quite a different matter. I am by no means certain that this counts as condoning a felony on my part.

It is possible that I am saving the game, and a great club, from disrepute. After all, it has been a wonderful match and we have no cause to tarnish it because a vile criminal was unfortunate enough to die during the day."

Mr Alcock approached Holmes with outstretched arms. "Mr Holmes, I have no words to demonstrate my gratitude."

Mr Beal got up from his seat as well. "I must say, Mr Holmes, I will be eternally indebted to you… "

Holmes waved the gracious words away with a casual waft of his hand. "The need of the hour is not words but action, my dear sirs. We must ensure that not a word that has been uttered in this room passes beyond these doors. Dr Watson here can accompany the two Grace brothers when they testify before Mr William Carter, the East Surrey coroner. With such a pantheon of noble witnesses, Mr Carter will have no cause to doubt that a heart ailment was indeed the cause of death. Watson, I hope that will not test your ethical standards as a medical practitioner."

"On the contrary, Holmes, it would test my commitment to the cause of cricket if I were to take any other course of action."

Mr Beal rushed forward and rung me by the hand. "I cannot tell you how indebted I am, Dr Watson. And of course, Mr Holmes. I invite you both to watch the great matches at Adelaide during the Australian summer, when the England side play in our part of the world later this year. I believe young Bligh is taking a team, Mr Alcock?"

Relief had spread across Mr Alcock's face, and was evidently surging through his expansive frame as well. He still sat on that iron safe, but now with his legs outstretched and his whole form relieved of the tautness and tension that had held it together throughout the day.

"Indeed it will be young Ivo. His father, the Earl of Darnley, is at this moment in the pavilion, congratulating Murdoch and his men."

We were surprised by a voice which rang out from behind us.

"Will that be all, Mr Holmes? Can I go now and explain the condition of the umbrella to my missus?"

All of us apart from Mr Beal burst out in unrestrained laughter, a blessed release after the multiple layers of excitement of the day. Mr Alcock was slowly returning to his own dapper, sociable self as secretary of the Surrey County Cricket Club.

"Mr Beal, our brave bookmaker here," he said, turning to Courcy, "tried to tamper with the evidence, all for your sake. He chewed clean through his umbrella to destroy the bloodstain."

"I couldn't help but do that, gentlemen. The moment I saw Mr Holmes walk into the stand and examine the spot where Spenlow had fallen down to his death, I knew I had to do something. He has a reputation among us. I could not very well get rid of the umbrella, because several of the spectators had seen me with it, even taken shelter under it when it was raining. I did once think of leaving the ground and making a run for it, but then, sirs, I could not very well stay away when there was this great match going on, could I now?"

Mr Beal held Courcy by the hand and looked at him warmly. "It is your loyalty to cricket that helped to keep Spenlow from spoiling this great game, Courcy. And I may very well add that it is for this same reason that you will never become a successful bookmaker. Never you mind that, my good man, there are plenty of things in this life other than success."

"Well, sir, there is of course cricket. But, I would like to hear you to name four more things."

Mr Beal laughed heartily and led Courcy by the arm. "You can run along to tell the wife about your umbrella, as long as you don't breathe a word of what actually happened. But before that you can come into the club room and enjoy the celebrations."

Courcy stood transfixed, almost unable to believe what he had just heard. He passed his tongue over his lips.

"You mean that, Mr Beal, sir? In the pavilion with Grace, Hornby, Murdoch and The Demon himself?"

"Yes, my man. Mr Holmes, Dr Watson, please join me as well."

Beal opened the door but could not proceed any further, for at that very moment there stepped in a lean and ferret like man, furtive and sly in appearance.

"I was told Mr Alcock is in here," he said, as he looked at us in some surprise.

It was an unexpected shock to find Inspector Lestrade with us in the room all of a sudden, regarding us with his keen eyes. It was abundantly clear within a few moments that the surprise was mutual. Sherlock Holmes was the last person Lestrade had expected to find on entering the Surrey committee room in the pavilion of The Oval.

"Mr Holmes, I must say this is a surprise."

"Yes, Lestrade, we are here as the guests of Mr Alcock, the gentleman you are looking for. It has been proposed, if you must know, for Watson to become a member of the Surrey Committee."

"I never knew you gentlemen were so interested in cricket."

Charles Alcock looked at the Inspector from Scotland Yard with a distinct lack of friendliness.

"They were my honoured guests for this excellent match. Now, Inspector, to what do we owe your visit?"

Lestrade bowed slightly. "I do beg your pardon, sir, but I believe a man called Spenlow died today in the ground, and was treated here in the pavilion before being sent to the Bart in an ambulance."

"That's right, there was a sick man, but he was dead by the time to the pavilion. And we never learnt his name. We had four doctors examining him. Dr Watson here, EM Grace and WG himself, and finally Dr Jones, President of the Club. All of them agreed that it was a weak heart that led to the sudden attack."

Lestrade's eyes turned a shade reverential as he listened. "WG himself examined the man? He must have been right. I came here because Spenlow has been a known member of London's underworld, and I had to ascertain there was no foul play involved."

"Come on, man, what foul business can take place on a cricket ground?" Mr Alcock sounded rather annoyed. "If one watches such a close game with a weak heart, one has a good chance of falling dead. I'm sure his doctors would have warned him against it."

Lestrade nodded and bowed again.

"I'm sure of that. So sorry to disturb you, sir. Give my regards to Dr Grace. I hear he did not win today, but he will remain our Champion."

The Inspector had been about to leave when he suddenly stopped in his tracks. Beside me, I could see Holmes stiffen. "Watson," he whispered. "I think you are standing here beside the greatest fool in Europe, and I say that even when we have Lestrade less than twenty feet away. I should have cleared it up long ago. The Inspector is bone-headed, but he will definitely suspect something now."

Indeed, the glance of this member of the police force had fallen on the tobacco ash laid out on the small piece of cloth on the table, which Holmes had used in unravelling the sequence of strange events that had taken place earlier in the day.

"What's that?" Lestrade asked, pointing.

"Come now, Watson, you are the writer. Make something up quickly."

Lestrade looked from face to face. "Mr Holmes, I've worked with you often enough to know that you consider yourself an expert on tobacco ash, and have a theory that evidence of that sort helps in solving cases."

"I don't just have a theory, Lestrade. If you can yourself think back to the case of Jefferson Hope, the Trichinopoly ash did play a big role in clearing up the details. But this is a completely different matter altogether."

Lestrade looked at the table again, frowning at the contents.

"What is that then?"

"Watson?" prompted Holmes.

"Ashes," said I.

There was silence for a while before Lestrade laughed menacingly. "I know it's ashes, Dr Watson, but what's it doing on the table?"

I forced myself into deep thought, trying to figure out a logical explanation, and suddenly there was inspiration. Perhaps my days in India had a part to play in it.

"Have you watched the match today, Mr Lestrade?"

"No, I haven't. I hear it was a close thing, but I was busy, fighting crime, you see."

"Well, England had to score 85 runs to win, and were 51 for 2 at one point. And then they collapsed to 77 all out. We have decided, in our committee meeting here, that English cricket is dead, Mr Lestrade. The foreigners will take away the ashes."

Lestrade looked from one face to another.

"What in God's name is that supposed to mean?"

"Why, Mr Lestrade, this is a memento of the great match. These are the ashes of our great English game. When England goes to Australia next, they will be competing with a representative side to bring back these very ashes."

Lestrade's face underwent some contortion as he grappled strenuously with this fantastic bit of made-up nonsense.

"You mean this is going to be some sort of a prize?"

"Yes sir, a trophy. We are going to put the whole thing in an urn, and the Australians are going to carry it back home. From now on the representative matches between England and Australia are going to be known as The Ashes. That's what they will be playing for."

Mr Alcock interjected now. "Well, the Australian cricketers don't know yet. ... I have my friend Sir William Clarke living in London at present, a noted pastoralist and philanthropist who lives in the charming mansion Rupertswood. ... We have heard he may soon be made a baronet by the Queen. Bligh, who leads the next team to Australia, will be staying a fair amount of time with him in Rupertswood, for ... well ... for various reasons. I will ask Sir William to take charge of the urn and young Ivo can bring it back if he wins the series of representative matches."

Lestrade was still trying to figure it out.

"The Honourable Ivo Bligh?"

"Yes, his father, the Earl of Darnley, is now in the pavilion. As is Lord Harris."

At the mention of these august members of the aristocracy, Lestrade paused in thought.

"What have you burnt to make those ashes now?"

"A ball," replied Mr Alcock.

"A bail," said Mr Beal.

"Both the match ball and the match bail," said Holmes.

Lestrade stood blinking for a few moments before he shrugged. "All this for a game of cricket? Well, sirs, I'll leave you to it."

The Inspector withdrew to the general relief of everyone in the room.

"Tell you what, Mr Beal," Courcy offered in a shaky voice. "I will give the Graces and the Spoffs a miss. My every nerve and sinew tells me that the best course of action for me will be to get out of The Oval as soon as possible."

Very seldom have I witnessed Holmes tickled so much by the mirth of the situation. He slapped Courcy on the back, laughing, "Come now, Mr Courcy. Lestrade is one of the smartest of the force. Although that is not saying much, if we have put him off the trail there is not much else to fear."

CHAPTER 14

THE LEGEND

MR ALCOCK led the way with a thoughtful expression on his face.

"Mr Holmes, while the Inspector has been deceived for now, the ruse must be maintained. We have to act in haste to create this legend of The Ashes. If not, there may yet be suspicions floating around."

Walking out of the committee room and into the revelry outside, Holmes sounded unusually jovial.

"The Press, Mr Alcock, is the most valuable institution, if only you know how to use it. There is a lot to be said for the press-box in the adjacent building, isn't there, with every reporter eager to denigrate the same England team they praised to the heavens yesterday? Go, Mr Alcock, take Watson with you and get the news of the Ashes into the newspapers."

"I am afraid, Mr Holmes, the hour is late, and the pressmen must have all left while we were engaged in the committee room."

A dapper man with long whiskers paused as he was passing us.

"No, Alcock, some haven't."

"You say some are still there? Have you seen them, Buns?"

I realised we were speaking to Mr Charles Thornton.

"I just ran into young Reggie Brookes of the *Sporting Times*. He was so caught up in the excitement that he had forgotten to telegraph his report. He was rushing back to the press-box. If you hasten along, you will be in time to grab him."

Mr Alcock strode into the club room, beckoning me to follow. As we entered, Spofforth got down from the centre table, having completed what, judging by the reactions of the gathering, had been a rousing speech. The Demon's eyes seemed almost mellow now and rather full of mirth. I could meet them without having the dreadful feeling of having my internal organs both scrutinised and scorched.

"Spoff," remarked Mr Alcock. "You must repeat whatever you said word for word. I did not manage to catch anything of it."

The great bowler laughed good-naturedly, "Sorry, Mr Alcock, I was not listening to myself either. I don't remember a word I said."

Just as we were stepping out of the room, making for the stairs, we came across the form of an old gentleman, drooping over his seat, in an alarming posture of resignation. Mr Alcock paused and touched him on the back, "Is anything the matter, Mr Fitzgerald?"

The old man rose, revealing himself to be none other than my companion through most of Australia's innings in the morning.

"Oh no, Mr Alcock. Only I don't know whether to cry or be sick. You see, sir, had Caffyn or Caesar or Lockyer been there …"

"Quick Mr Watson, we may be too late …," Mr Alcock shot through the doors like a bolt of lightning.

Descending the steps the first person we came across was poor Ted Peate.

"I say Ted, why on earth didn't you block and let Studd score the runs?" demanded Mr Alcock gruffly.

The Yorkshire bowler looked at us with morose eyes peering over his drooping moustache.

"I couldn't trust Mr Studd, sir."

With an appeal to the heavens, Mr Alcock made for the press box.

***

Two days had passed since I had shaken the huge, strong hand of WG and, alongside him and EM, had given the evidence upon which the Coroner of East Surrey, William Carter, had pronounced a verdict of death by natural causes in the case of Mr James Spenlow. Of course, we did not discuss the circumstances, and even if the Graces did know about the sensational incidents on that fateful day, they made no mention of them.

I had no doubt that even if they had been aware of the occurrences, the two brothers would not have strayed from their statements. WG not only lived for the game, but was himself for all intents and purposes the very face of the game. Besides, EM Grace had voyaged to Australia some two decades earlier, with the team under George Parr of Nottinghamshire, and still remembered the visit as some of the best and most fulfilling days of his life. Neither of them was likely to utter one word which might imperil the cricketing relations between England and Australia.

We now sat in our Baker Street rooms, the early September already experiencing gales of such violence that we had to keep the windows locked against the elemental forces.

I was buried in the *Sporting Times* in which the following announcement appeared under the name of Bloobs, the pseudonym of young Reginald Shirley Brooks.

"In Affectionate Remembrance
OF
ENGLISH CRICKET,
WHICH DIED AT THE OVAL
ON
29TH AUGUST, 1882,
Deeply lamented by a large circle of sorrowing
friends and acquaintances
R.I.P.
N.B. — The body will be cremated and the ashes
taken to Australia."

Sherlock Holmes, who was stretched out with his feet on the corner of the mantelpiece, was reading the day's paper, looking at the short report of a man who had dropped dead of a weak heart at The Oval.

"With time, Watson, I can see this legend of The Ashes taking hold of the public imagination. It is so with many such elements of the so-called news which we consider to be unequivocally true. As I mentioned, the very words of the newspapers that the gullible public take to be facts can be manipulated to give a false account. Cricket is no exception, and with time and popularity many such fictional elements will be considered as part of the game's authentic history. Mark my words, Watson, a hundred years from now, when time has sprinkled its gold dust, men will look back to this great cricket match played at The Oval in August 1882 as those good old days when the game was honourable and money and professionalism had not been allowed to tarnish the good old spirit."

On that day, I had protested, saying that my friend had too low an opinion of the public. But in the coming years, perhaps the carefully manicured memories of men such as Lord Harris – or some spectator fondly recalling the days of Hornby and Barlow in lofty verse – will create an unduly idealised sense of a Golden Age of Cricket. If so, the ancient words of Holmes will reverberate with wisdom transcending time.

APPENDIX 1

THE SCORECARD

England v Australia

Australia in British Isles 1882 (Only Test)

Venue: Kennington Oval, Kennington on 28th, 29th August 1882 (3-day match)

Balls per over: 4

Toss: Australia won the toss and decided to bat

Umpires: L Greenwood, RA Thoms

Close of play day 1: England (1) 101 all out

Australia first innings

		Rs	Bs	Mins	4s	6s
AC Bannerman	c Grace b Peate	9	86	70	-	-
HH Massie	b Ulyett	1	4	7	-	-
*WL Murdoch	b Peate	13	70	50	1	-
GJ Bonnor	b Barlow	1	6	5	-	-
TP Horan	b Barlow	3	18	20	-	-
G Giffen	b Peate	2	23	17	-	-
+JM Blackham	c Grace b Barlow	17	51	40	2	-
TW Garrett	c Read b Peate	10	34	25	-	-
HF Boyle	b Barlow	2	10	5	-	-
SP Jones	c Barnes b Barlow	0	14	12	-	-
FR Spofforth	not out	4	4	3	1	-
Extras	(1 b)	1				
Total	**(all out, 80 overs)**	**63**				

Fall of wickets:

1-6 (Massie), 2-21 (Murdoch), 3-22 (Bonnor), 4-26 (Bannerman), 5-30 (Horan), 6-30 (Giffen), 7-48 (Garrett), 8-53 (Boyle), 9-59 (Blackham), 10-63 (Jones, 80 ov)

England bowling

	Ovs	Ms	Runs	Wkts	Ws	NBs
Peate	38	24	31	4	-	-
Ulyett	9	5	11	1	-	-
Barlow	31	22	19	5	-	-
Steel	2	1	1	0	-	-

England first innings

		Rs	Bs	Mins	4s	6s
RG Barlow	c Bannerman b Spofforth	11	35	30	-	-
WG Grace	b Spofforth	4	15	20	-	-
G Ulyett	st Blackham b Spofforth	26	64	55	1	-
AP Lucas	c Blackham b Boyle	9	64	65	1	-
+A Lyttelton	c Blackham b Spofforth	2	20	25	-	-
CT Studd	b Spofforth	0	3	2	-	-
JM Read	not out	19	42	45	2	-
W Barnes	b Boyle	5	10	9	1	-
AG Steel	b Garrett	14	24	22	1	-
*AN Hornby	b Spofforth	2	9	5	-	-
E Peate	c Boyle b Spofforth	0	2	1	-	-
Extras	(6 b, 2 lb, 1 nb)	9				
Total	**(all out, 71.3 overs)**	**101**				

Fall of wickets:

1-13 (Grace), 2-18 (Barlow), 3-57 (Ulyett), 4-59 (Lucas), 5-60 (Studd), 6-63 (Lyttelton), 7-70 (Barnes), 8-96 (Steel), 9-101 (Hornby), 10-101 (Peate, 71.3 ov)

Australia bowling

	Ovs	Ms	Runs	Wkts	Ws	NBs
Spofforth	36.3	18	46	7	-	1
Garrett	16	7	22	1	-	-
Boyle	19	7	24	2	-	-

Australia second innings

		Rs	Bs	Mins	4s	6s
AC Bannerman	c Studd b Barnes	13	61	70	-	-
HH Massie	b Steel	55	62	57	9	-
GJ Bonnor	b Ulyett	2	9	9	-	-
*WL Murdoch	run out	29	60	70	1	-
TP Horan	c Grace b Peate	2	6	10	-	-
G Giffen	c Grace b Peate	0	1	1	-	-
+JM Blackham	c Lyttelton b Peate	7	15	13	1	-
SP Jones	run out	6	29	30	1	-
FR Spofforth	b Peate	0	5	3	-	-
TW Garrett	not out	2	4	5	-	-
HF Boyle	b Steel	0	1	1	-	-
Extras	(6 b)	6				
Total	**(all out, 63 overs)**	**122**				

Fall of wickets:

1-66 (Massie), 2-70 (Bonnor), 3-70 (Bannerman), 4-79 (Horan), 5-79 (Giffen), 6-99 (Blackham), 7-114 (Jones), 8-117 (Spofforth), 9-122 (Murdoch), 10-122 (Boyle, 63 ov)

England bowling

	Ovs	Ms	Runs	Wkts	Ws	NBs
Barlow	13	5	27	0	-	-
Ulyett	6	2	10	1	-	-
Peate	21	9	40	4	-	-
Studd	4	1	9	0	-	-
Barnes	12	5	15	1	-	-
Steel	7	0	15	2	-	-

England second innings

		Rs	Bs	Mins	4s	6s
WG Grace	c Bannerman b Boyle	32	52	55	2	-
*AN Hornby	b Spofforth	9	17	16	1	-
RG Barlow	b Spofforth	0	1	1	-	-
G Ulyett	c Blackham b Spofforth	11	28	32	1	-
AP Lucas	b Spofforth	5	55	65	1	-
+A Lyttelton	b Spofforth	12	54	50	1	-
AG Steel	c and b Spofforth	0	3	4	-	-
JM Read	b Spofforth	0	2	1	-	-
W Barnes	c Murdoch b Boyle	2	6	6	-	-
CT Studd	not out	0	2	5	-	-
E Peate	b Boyle	2	3	1	-	-
Extras	(3 b, 1 nb)	4				
Total	**(all out, 55 overs)**	**77**				

Fall of wickets:

1-15 (Hornby), 2-15 (Barlow), 3-51 (Ulyett), 4-53 (Grace), 5-66 (Lyttelton), 6-70 (Steel), 7-70 (Read), 8-75 (Lucas), 9-75 (Barnes), 10-77 (Peate, 55 ov)

Australia bowling

	Ovs	Ms	Runs	Wkts	Ws	NBs
Spofforth	28	15	44	7	-	1
Garrett	7	2	10	0	-	-
Boyle	20	11	19	3	-	-

Result: Australia won by 7 runs

* The rules in 1882 permitted a bowler to change ends once in an innings by bowling two consecutive overs. Spofforth took advantage of this clause in both the innings.

APPENDIX 2

SHERLOCK HOLMES and John Watson met in 1881. That was the year when Watson witnessed the extraordinary powers of deduction of his new friend in the adventures documented in *A Study in Scarlet*.

The following year, 1882, saw the great contest at The Oval, when WG Grace and Fred Spofforth clashed in one of the most riveting matches ever played, and it gave birth to the legend of the Ashes.

If we look at the account left by Watson, 1882 was a rather idle year for the great detective. Or was it? Or were there tales for which 'the world was not yet prepared'? Did Holmes have something to do with the birth of the Ashes legend?

It was a delight to bring to light the sensational events at The Oval on that August day of 1882, and describe how Sherlock Holmes played a defining part in creating one of the lasting traditions of English cricket.

Stepping aside from the Great Game (in all senses) let me take the opportunity here to note that the events that take place in the novel, the action and the dialogue, in the playing arena and the pavilion, are very close to what actually occurred that day.

From Hornby's introduction of Ulyett to counter the big hitting ability of Bonnor, to Charles Alcock's dazed gesture of sitting on the iron safe after the conclusion of the match, to the Surrey member's wail of despair 'I don't know whether to cry or be sick' ... everything actually took place on that day. The events described during the voyage of the Australians have also been kept as close to the documented details of the times as possible. The involvement of Holmes and Watson are built into the sequence, and remain true to the timelines, individual characteristics etc. as outlined in the canon and agreed to by various Holmesian scholars. Some of the historically accurate dialogue take place as responses to statements by Holmes or Watson.

The discerning reader will find some parts where Holmes and Watson repeat words and phrases, indeed sentiments, that are common in the canon. But then, that can be attributed to characteristic. Besides, it is often impossible to find expressions as good as the ones used by the master Sir Arthur Conan Doyle.

ABOUT THE AUTHOR

Arunabha Sengupta is a Cricket Historian and Chief Cricket Writer at cricketcountry.com. He is also the author of three previous novels: *Labyrinth - a Novel about the Software Industry*, *Big Apple 2 Bites* and *The Best Seller.*

BOULDER ROLLING
TOM SMITH'S 2015 DIARY
A Story of Courage, Determination and Resiliance

The contrast between Tom Smith's 2014 and 2015 seasons could not have been starker. In 2014 the all-rounder enjoyed the best personal season of his career to gain England Lions recognition and then dominate Lancashire's end of season awards after being named both the Championship Player of the Year and the overall Player of the Year.

He took 54 wickets and hit 773 runs in County Championship matches and his quick scoring at the top of the order was an integral part of Lancashire's success in reaching the NatWest T20 Blast final, earning selection for the Lions' one-day series against the A sides of New Zealand and Sri Lanka in August. To cap a memorable year, Tom married fiancée Holly in December 2014.

Tom's 2015 started well when he was named Lancashire captain for 2015 and it was a proud moment when he led the team out at Derby to start the new season. And then it all went horribly wrong.

Injuries never arrive at a good time in a player's career, but it to be side-lined after leading your team for one match was particularly cruel. Tom's response was to fight back hard, but it took him to the limit-and beyond.

'Boulder rolling' is a phrase frequently banded around the Lancashire dressing room to put some momentum behind a success. In Tom's case it represented a motivation to comeback from a potential career-ending injury, and one which tested his courage, resilience and patience, to new limits.

During his rehabilitation, Tom kept a diary throughout 2015 to help him chart his progress. As a result Boulder Rolling is an extremely honest and, at times, eye-opening account of what it is really like for a professional sportsman to be out of action with a serious injury.

Tom also provides a narrative on Lancashire's spectacularly successful 2015 season, albeit one from inside the dressing room, which saw the team gain promotion to the First Division of the County Championship and win the NatWest T20 Blast trophy.

Twelve months after experiencing the disappointment of losing the 2014 T20 final, Tom found himself back on the pitch at Edgbaston celebrating Lancashire's success with the rest of the team. The irony wasn't lost on him, but by then Tom's own boulder was rolling in the right direction…….

Price £9 post free from:

Max Books. Epworth House 34 Wellington Road, Nantwich, Cheshire CW5 7BX.

A publisher specialising in Books on Lancashire Cricket and Crime/Detection stories.

Also Limited edition books on Lancashire Cricket. Please apply for more details.

www.max-books.co.uk